I0452910

TIME TAMPER

BY

Nancy J MacLean

TIME TAMPER, published by Fredbagel Books (Nancy J MacLean)
Njmacleanauthor.webs.com

Print version ISBN: 978-0-9921190-0-3
Electronic version ISBN: 978-0-9921190-1-0

To my late husband Don, who always supported my foolishness. And to Dave and Trish, who continue to do so.

ONE

Wausau, Wisconsin, August 5, 1962

The first thing Kenneth O'Neil would be able to remember was an image of the right rear fin of a car cutting through the river's surface like a shark. It wasn't until the red triangle of the taillight disappeared that he realized someone was about to die.

Panic pushed him into motion. He scrambled down the pebbled embankment and waded into the cold, black water. After only a few feet, its icy depths impeded his forward motion. He inhaled and dove. The frigid temperature threatened to steal his breath but he fiercely held onto it, knowing that during the next minute every molecule of oxygen would become precious.

The car's mangled nose dug into the riverbed. Clouds of murk billowed upward. The automobile twisted sideways and the screech of crumpling metal, magnified by the water, assaulted Ken's eardrums. A jagged shard of metal snagged the right flap of his jacket and pulled him up and over the car. He twisted out of his jacket and, using it as towline, pulled himself toward the shiny strip he hoped was the door handle. He pulled on it.

The door was jammed.

He freed a few bubbles of air from his lungs, then peered through the window but could see nothing through the dark water. More air escaped from his aching lungs as he yanked on the door. He managed to open it a few inches. Another tug resulted in a gap a foot wide. He squeezed his upper torso into the car and prayed for a pocket of air. There was none. He felt along the front seat but found nothing. He could not reach into the back. The last of his air left in a burst of bubbles and he knew he had to surface or die.

His oxygen-deprived brain struggled to determine which direction was up. The water above him seemed endless. As the cold sapped his body heat, his limbs grew leaden. A choice came to him. He could relax. Give up. End the sadness. But a thought nagged him. There was something he had to do.

Something important.

Save the driver, of course.

No, that wasn't it.

Was it common to argue with oneself when on the verge of drowning?

Suddenly he broke through into glorious fresh air. He gulped, swallowed water, choked, coughed, then took another breath. The current swept him along. White water frothed around him. His knees scraped bottom, but he could not get a footing. He tumbled into a rock, but could not grip its eely surface before the river tossed him onward.

He heard a shout. There, downstream a figure stood on the bank. He tried to angle toward it but fatigue would not let him. No longer cold, he only wanted to sleep. Let the river have its way. But again, he felt there was something important he had to do.

The river slowed and the water grew deep again, but it was difficult to stay afloat. The figure loomed ahead of him and leaned forward, one arm extended. Ken took as deep a breath as he could force into his shrunken lungs, then attempted to stroke towards the shore, arm over arm. Arm over arm. With each movement awkward and broken, the river controlled him like a marionette. He had no idea what his legs were doing.

A hand reached out, the palm up.

But he could do no more.

Water swallowed the hand and darkness swallowed him.

* * *

"Ow!" Someone pinched the little finger of Ken's right hand hard enough to spread pain into his palm.

"Sir?"

Ken struggled to open eyelids that weighed tons. The bright light forced him to squint. Two men stood at the bedside. The one in the white lab coat was tall and slim with dark hair except for patches of grey at the temples. The man beside him was obviously a law officer of some kind. He was older, shorter, and a little heavy about the middle.

The officer started to speak, but the lab coat interrupted him. "I'm Dr. White and this is Sergeant Stevens. You are in Memorial Hospital. You nearly drowned."

The police officer leaned past the doctor. "You had no identification on you. Is there someone we can contact to let them know you're all right?"

Was there? Ken took a slow breath and waited for the answer to come to him. It did. "No." At least that felt like the right answer.

"What's your name?" Sergeant Stevens asked.

Surely he knew the answer to this question. Surely . . . Ken inhaled deeply to stem a tide of nausea and studied the room, but the austere walls and pale blue curtains told him nothing.

"Sir…?" the sergeant prodded.

Ken's throat tightened beneath the grip of panic. "I – I don't know," he answered honestly.

The doctor patted Ken's shoulder. "You were unconscious when the sergeant here pulled you from the water. Amnesia after such an event is not unusual and, in most cases, it's temporary." The doctor handed Ken a mirror and smiled. "Maybe you'll recognize this fellow."

The image that stared back at Ken looked vaguely familiar, yet not quite right. He appeared to be in his forties. Not an overly handsome man and his short haircut revealed a receding hairline. His black eyes shone with an alertness that was quickly being consumed by anxiety. He tossed the mirror onto the bed and shook his head.

"May we ask you a few more questions?" the doctor asked. "They might prompt your memory."

"Sure," Ken said although he didn't really want to learn just how much he didn't know. Not knowing was just too scary. He'd rather they just let him go to sleep so he could wake up from this nightmare.

"Do you know today's date?"

Another scrutiny of the room failed to provide an answer. Ken gave his head another shake.

The doctor scribbled on a clipboard. "Do you know what city you are in?"

At last an answer popped into Ken's head. "Washington?"

Their sympathetic gazes informed him this was wrong.

"Wausau, Wisconsin," the sergeant said in a soft voice that offered conspiracy.

The doctor frowned and cleared his throat. "Let's start with what you *do* remember."

Ken opened his mind. His stomach tightened at the nothingness he found there. "I-I'm sorry."

"Do you remember anything about the accident?"

"Accident?" Vivid images of the car in the river returned to him. With relief, he related his rescue attempt. He finished with, "But there was no one in the front seat. I didn't have time to see if there was anyone in the back." Survivor guilt bore down on him.

The sergeant quickly spoke up. "The divers found the car empty. The windshield was smashed out, so the driver could have been swept downstream. The Wisconsin River runs ragged at that point." Here he paused. "Did you know the driver?"

"No . . . at least I don't think I did."

"Do you remember what you were doing there by the river bank?"

Ken returned the direct look. "Sergeant, I wish I knew. But honestly, I have no idea. Were there any witnesses?"

The sergeant nodded. "There were two families picnicking at the park. They saw the Chevy crash through the rail of the bridge and into the river. Witnesses saw you dive in afterwards. By all accounts, you're a hero."

This did not assuage Ken's feeling of guilt. "But I didn't save anyone. Do you know who was driving the car?"

The sergeant nodded. "The plates show the car belonged to an Edward Smith." He paused and tapped his fingers on his ample abdomen. "Does the name ring any bells?"

Ken thought for a moment. "No. You're really the only hero here, Sergeant. Thanks for saving my life."

"I was near the park when the call came through. We've had a few rambunctious teenagers attempt to tame the rapids at various times. That cove is the only place to collect them before the river turns murderous. I headed straight there when I heard a car had gone in. We'll put word out to the papers and radio stations about you, both here and in Washington, and see if anyone who knows you comes forward."

No one will. The certainty behind the thought jolted Ken. How could he know this when he knew so little else? He rubbed his head.

"Do you have a headache?" the doctor asked.

"Yeah," Ken lied. But he didn't like the taste of it and quickly added, "No, not really. I'm just tired, and frankly these questions are scaring the shit out of me." There. The truth felt right. Whoever he was must be honest.

Dr. White turned to the sergeant. "Why don't we let him rest and see what he remembers in the morning?" He turned back to Ken and pointed to a bell on the bedside table. "Just ring if you need anything. Your nurse will be in to check on you periodically."

Sergeant Stevens leaned over the bed. "You just take it easy, son. Everything will be all right."

The gesture and words comforted Ken. "Thank you."

When the light went out Ken drank the darkness in, and felt even safer when he closed his eyes.

This is not real, he thought. Just some weird dream. Soon I'll wake up, remember everything, and laugh at the whole thing.

The feeling that none of these would really happen haunted him until fatigue won over and sleep reclaimed him.

TWO

Beijing, China, March 13, 2049

Hwang Ko gracefully unfolded his long legs out of the lotus position and headed for the shower. He stepped inside the cubicle and pushed the button to activate the twenty jets of hot water. Steam filled his world, and he wondered if this in any way resembled what it would be like in the time chambers when they sent him to 1962.

A draft tickled his back as the glass door opened and closed behind him. Willowy arms wound about his waist in gentle contrast to what he knew they were capable of. Shimira's teeth bit into the skin over his shoulder blade and pulled, hard enough to cause a sliver of delicious pain, but not enough to leave a mark.

He would have one more physical exam in the next few days and he did not want any new wounds that would raise questions. The scars on his body had always been explained as injuries from hand-to-hand combat. Most of them were not from fighting, but only he and Shimira knew that.

He leaned past her and pushed another button that changed the jets to a hot mist. He reached for the sponge and began to wash her.

She reached up to rest her hands on his shoulders. "Your American father must have been a tall, muscular man."

He was not surprised Shimira knew his past. She had the highest level of security clearance and had probably accessed his file right after they'd met, as he had hers.

Her words made him think of his mother. She was only twenty-one when she left the Chinese province of Korea to become a spy for Chinese Intelligence. After being captured in Italy, she was raped by an American agent. By the time she was freed, she was too far along in the pregnancy for an abortion, and she returned home to Korea to give birth. She died within an hour of bringing Ko into the world.

Shimira took the sponge and soaped him slowly, carefully.

He smiled down at her. "You can be so gentle . . . at times."

She stood on her toes and kissed him. "And you, too. But we are very different, Ko. You love the feel of pain, whereas I enjoy delivering it."

She looked up at him, her eyes large with an uncharacteristic wistfulness. "I wish they were sending someone else."

"I'm coming back," Ko said, touched at her worry. "They have already chosen my exchange subject, a reclusive farmer outside of Mauston. After the transfer they will keep him healthy to ensure my safe return."

He tapped her delicate nose then pushed the dryer button, and within a minute they were both fully dry.

Shimira exited first and began to pull on her issued jumpsuit. She wasn't looking at him, but he noted tension in her movements.

"What's wrong?" he asked.

She looked up. "The man the Americans sent to alter history, this Kenneth O'Neil. There wasn't much in his file. His wife and daughter died in a terrorist attack. A man with nothing to lose can be dangerous."

Ko laughed. "He's just a historian, recruited to tutor Lieutenant Peter Michaels. O'Neil's not even an agent."

"Then why did the Americans send him?"

Ko went to her and pulled open the zipper she had just began to close, exposing her toned abdomen. He traced a circle about her navel. "You know why. Michaels killed himself before you could get your hands on him and they had to send someone."

Shimira made a face at either his words, or his action, maybe both, but she left her uniform open. "But why not send another experienced agent?"

"We were already at their bunker's door. They probably didn't have a choice. Right after they sent O'Neil they tried to destroy the time chambers. Fortunately, we got to them before they could do too much damage."

"Will our scientists be able to bring O'Neil back?"

Ko shook his head. "No. His exchange subject died when we attacked the bunker. Why?"

She ran a finger down his bare chest, her long nail not quite scratching his skin. "Because I wanted to play with him, not like you, who prefers to deliver death quickly, cleanly." Her dark eyes narrowed. "For someone who enjoys pain so much, you never want others to suffer, do you?"

Ko inwardly flinched but did not turn away from her scrutiny. It was against protocol for them to be lovers and they had been diligent in keeping their affair a secret. As a result, he had never spent more than a few hours with her at a time. Yet he felt closer to Shimira than anyone, including his grandparents. However, with this last comment he worried she might be getting to know him a little too well.

"My grandmother suffered horribly with arthritis. It was hard to see her go through that." He hesitated, not sure what else he wanted to add.

"I know," Shimira said. She zipped up the front of her uniform, stopping where her perfect collarbones met her sternum. "You loved your grandparents."

She sat down on the bed, pulled on her boots, and began to lace them. When she said nothing further, Ko wondered how much she actually knew. He felt no guilt at how he had expedited his grandparents' deaths. Just as he felt no remorse when he killed those who were a threat to China. He prided himself on his swift, nearly painless executions.

Shimira stood up and pulled on her cap. She looked so beautiful he wanted to rip her uniform off.

The look in her eye told him she wanted him to do just that. But she had to report in. "The scientists predict the chambers will be repaired in a matter of weeks. Perhaps we will see each other once more before you leave."

"I hope so," he whispered.

She stepped close. "You are my hero, Ko. China's hero. You will stop O'Neil from tampering with time. You will protect history, ensuring China's supreme rule." She said all this as if it were already fact not supposition.

She spoke softly. "And then you will return to me."

She kissed him. They both kept their arms at their sides. Only their lips touched.

But that kiss was enough to make Ko yearn for just one more opportunity to make love to her before he journeyed to 1962.

THREE

Mauston, Wisconsin, August 5, 1962

Louise Jensen peered through the window. While silence reigned inside the empty house, nature partied outside. The wind tangoed with two large oaks in the front yard. Pregnant clouds approached rapidly from the west and she soon expected to hear the accompanying thunder.

She studied the half glass of wine in her hand. She hoped the drink would elevate her mood, but so far it hadn't. She twirled the glass and small pieces of cork danced on the surface.

A sudden throb in her right wrist drew her gaze to the brace she wore except when in bed. Eight years and she still abhorred the look of it. A car accident had resulted in a maimed right wrist and hand that required multiple surgeries and several months of difficult rehabilitation. Since then she had learned to use her left hand for almost everything, even writing. Some tasks still proved challenging, like removing the cork from a bottle of wine.

Whack! A large branch collided with the window.

Lou jumped back and wine slopped onto her hand. Bits of debris flew past the window, hurried onward by the strengthening wind. Perhaps she should light a candle in case the lights went out. A warm bath and a good book would go nicely with candlelight, she thought, and headed up the stairs.

Her son Matt had gone to the drive-in with his girlfriend Sandra. More than likely it didn't matter if it stormed or not. He would be leaving for West Point in two weeks and she doubted the two were paying attention to any movie that was playing. He had no curfew and she did not expect him home for a couple of hours.

The loneliness she felt at the moment was nothing compared to the emptiness she would feel after Matt left for West Point. After her husband, Ted, died in the Korean war, she had focused on providing for her son and teaching. When Matt left, would she lose half of her sense of self?

She went up the stairs and paused outside Matt's room. She rarely went in, except to look for missing towels. But lately she found herself straying there more frequently, wanting to embed the feeling of his presence in her head.

Chaos greeted her the moment she turned on the light. You want to remember this? she thought as she picked a path through the mess of T-shirts, jeans, and books to the only organized spot in the room: his painting desk and easel. Lou picked up a stack of her son's paintings and carried it over to his bed. It was in order, most recent on top and earlier portraits on the bottom. As she studied each piece her trained eye picked up how much he had progressed in the past two years.

A flash of lightening was immediately followed by thunder so loud the window rattled. The lights went out and darkness enveloped her. Rain pelted against the glass, demanding entrance, as if it could sense how alone she was. She fumbled in Matt's bedside drawer for the flashlight she knew he kept there.

She turned it on and was about to leave the room when the lights came back on. She returned to the bed to put the portraits away. The one she had been about to look at was a sketch Matt had done of her shortly after he'd first started drawing. It was one of his first charcoal attempts - not really a good likeness. But he had done a good job with the eyes; they just didn't look like hers. She gathered the paintings and sketches and carefully put them back.

The array of paints and brushes on the desk made her yearn to paint again. She scowled as she tried to flex the fingers of her weak hand. Her ability to paint and her career as an artist had died in the car accident. The idea that she could teach what she loved to do came to her just recently. She talked the principal, Mrs. Wilson, into letting her teach an art course to the eighth graders in addition to her literature classes. It would use up her spare periods, but she wouldn't mind the extra work, especially with Matt not home.

The storm passed and by the time she crawled into bed a chilling quiet had replaced it, interspersed with the occasional creak of the floorboards.

She wished the wind had at least remained to keep her company.

But that too had moved on.

FOUR

Wausau, August 6, 1962

Ken woke to the gray light of dawn. It took a few minutes for his befuddled brain to remember the events of the previous night: the accident, waking up in the hospital, the nurse checking in on him every few hours. Beyond that . . . nothing. Then his amnesia was pierced by a solitary certainty.

There was something he had to do.

He sat up.

Pee. He had to pee. Although he sensed that wasn't it, at the moment his bladder had priority. Through the open doorway to his left he saw the porcelain curve of a sink. He threw off the sheets and searched for the button that would lower the bedrail. After another protest from his bladder he elected to crawl over. His stiff and bruised body reminded him of the few rounds he had lost to the river rocks.

When his bare feet touched the cold linoleum his bladder protested and threatened to empty right then and there. He dashed toward the bathroom but was brought up short by a tube that tethered him to a pole on the opposite side of the bed.

Ken groaned and holding himself like a two-year-old in training pants, he crawled back over the rail, into the bed, and out the other side. He had just landed on his feet when a voice boomed behind him.

"And what, sir, do you think you are doing?" A large nurse stood in the doorway. Her white uniform contrasted her ruddy features. Untamable red curls escaped the edges of her nurse's cap.

Dancing in spite of himself, Ken pointed helplessly to the bathroom.

With a soft laugh that did not fit her commanding voice, she pushed the intravenous pole toward him. He noticed it was on wheels.

"Do you need help?" she asked.

He shook his head and steered his way around the bed and through the narrow doorway. His rough navigation made the intravenous bottle swing precariously on its hook. Glass? What happened to plastic?

As he fumbled with the fabric of his gown he wondered how Scots managed with their kilts. He released his stream in a torrent and leaned in weakening bliss over the urinal. His happy bladder rejuvenated him and with a lighter step he turned to the sink and turned on the tap.

Ken glanced at the smiling stranger in the mirror. The man's smile vanished at eye contact. His hair was too short, he decided. He forced a grin to make the dimples return but it looked more like a grimace. He sighed, wiped his hands, and headed back, and nearly forgot to take the pole with him.

"Back so soon?" In his absence, the nurse had straightened his bed and the rails were lowered. "Did your bowels move?"

He felt himself blush. "N-no."

"Well, then, honey, you could have just used this." She pointed to a metal jug on the bedside table.

Now you tell me, he thought. "Where's the button to lower the rails?" Ken asked.

She frowned. "Button? Like on a shirt? No, you move this lever on the side and the rail slides up and down."

Although she demonstrated this easily enough, it didn't seem right to him.

But the nurse let the matter drop. "Now, how about we get you shaved, then see if the breakfast trays have arrived? Do you feel like you could eat something?"

Ken realized he was hungry. Ravenous, in fact. "Yes, please." He was surprised at how easily he could smile. And he liked the effect his smile had on the nurse.

Just as Ken polished off a second helping of eggs, toast, and oatmeal porridge, Sergeant Stevens walked through the door. He had clothes draped over one arm.

"Good morning, son." As he carefully laid the clothes over the back of the chair, he exposed a shoebox. This he set under the chair before he sat down.

The clothes were Ken's, freshly laundered and ironed. The smile he gave the policeman felt natural.

The alert blue eyes gave Ken the once over. "You look as if you're feeling better."

"I am, thank you."

"Do you remember anything else?"

Ken shook his head. A thought occurred to him. "Would it be possible to see a newspaper?"

"That's a good idea, son." The policeman jumped to his feet.

Dr. White entered at that moment. "Darn, it, Tom! What are you doing here so early? I wanted to assess him before you got at him again."

"I brought in his clothes and I was just goin' to fetch him a paper."

"The nurses will have one at the desk," the doctor said in dismissal, then turned to Ken. "How are you feeling?"

"Fine."

Dr. White picked up the chart from its hook on the end of the bed. "Nurse Benning said you were up and over the rails this morning. Any pain doing that?"

"Just a bit sore here and there."

"Well, that's to be expected." The doctor eyed the empty tray. "Appetite seems to have returned. It appears you are one lucky man."

Ken nodded. Nagged once again by the certainty there was something he had to do, he asked, "When can I be discharged?"

"I'm waiting on an orthopedic consult on your x-rays. Besides, where would you go?" The doctor regarded him warily.

Where *could* he go? "I don't know."

"Then perhaps you should let us keep an eye on you. Who knows, your memory might return, or someone might show up looking for you."

"I don't feel right taking up a hospital bed when I feel fine."

Dr. White shrugged. "We'll chat when the consults come in."

Before Ken could argue further, the sergeant returned and handed over a newspaper.

Ken opened the paper across his lap. "**MARILYN MUNROE DIES; PILLS BLAMED** " covered the top of the front page. His eyes darted to the date. "Monday, Aug. 6, 1962."

The date felt wrong and another round of panic began to stir in his gut.

"Do you remember who Marilyn Monroe was?" the sergeant asked.

"A movie star," Ken murmured in as normal a voice as he could manage.

"Good. Do you remember anything else?"

A few images and facts came into his head, but they were all about Marilyn, not himself. He wearily shook his head.

"I'll check back with you later," the doctor said. "Get the nurses to page me if you remember anything else."

The sergeant pulled up a chair and settled his large frame into it. He obviously planned to visit for a while.

Ken focused on the newspaper and ignored his quiet audience. Everything on the pages in front of him seemed wrong. He leaned back onto his pillow and allowed a sigh to escape.

"Hang in there, son," the sergeant said. "We're liable to hear from Washington any minute now. Some beautiful woman will probably come runnin' to claim you."

No. And no. They were certainties that led only to more questions, so he kept them to himself. As a diversion he focused on his visitor.

"Thank you for cleaning my clothes, Sergeant. Hope it wasn't too much of a bother."

"Call me Tom, son." The officer chuckled. "I have a wonderful wife who will always do me a favor."

Ken's curiosity washed aside the turmoil and he welcomed the respite though he knew it was only temporary. "Now why would your wife do something for a total stranger?"

The big man smiled easily with no sign of a hidden agenda. "What's wrong with giving a hand to a good person in need?"

"How do you know what kind of person I am?" Ken challenged and allowed a little of his frustration to show. "How can you tell, when I don't even know myself? You could be talking to a bank robber, a thief, or something worse."

Tom smiled, "Now, look, son. I've been a cop for nearly thirty years and I've met all shades of the people spectrum. I consider myself to be a good judge of character and I sense the man sitting in front of me is a good one."

Ken responded with a smile. "Well, thanks, Tom and thank Mrs. Stevens for me." He turned back to the paper and hoped some name or place would jump-start his memory.

Just as Ken reached the sports section, Nurse Benning came in to remove his intravenous line. He found he had to look away when she extracted the needle from his arm. He did not risk a peek until she had covered the site with gauze and tape. So now he knew something else about himself: he was a wimp.

Tom's eyes twinkled but he refrained from commenting.

After the nurse closed the door behind her Ken crawled out of bed.

"Now where you goin', son?" Tom asked.

"I'm too well to be here. Besides, I might remember something when I get outside." He began to pull on the neatly pressed clothes. Even his underwear looked as if it had been ironed.

When Ken was dressed, Tom handed him the box. Inside was a new pair of loafers. "The divers came up with only one of your shoes, so I got you a pair."

Ken straightened up and gave the policeman a direct look. "Tom, I don't know when or how I'm going to be able to —"

Tom cut him off in a rather stern voice. "Now, hold on, son, I ain't asking for repayment. Did you hear me ask for anything?" He stabbed a finger at him. "Now did you?"

Ken felt like he had just committed a misdemeanor. He swallowed, offered as charming a smile as he could muster, after all, it had worked on the nurse, and said, "No sir."

Tom's face relaxed and in a softer tone he said, "Then that's settled."

"But —"

Tom moved quicker than one would have thought possible and before Ken knew it, the policeman's finger was in his face again.

"Not another word. Now, where are you going to go?"

"Yes, where are you going?" Dr. White echoed the question as he came through the door.

The face Ken had studied in the mirror that morning had looked *at least* forty, maybe even forty-five. So why did he feel like an adolescent negotiating curfew?

He shrugged off the scrutiny of the two men and proceeded to tidy up the newspaper on his bed. "I'm not sure . . ." His eye caught the title of a short column at the bottom left of the sports page. It read: "Duluth Dukes Fail to Make Playoffs." It was about a minor league baseball team. Duluth. The name stuck in his brain.

"Duluth," he said aloud, then turned triumphantly back to Tom and Dr. White. "Something tells me to go to Duluth."

"Duluth, Minnesota?" Dr. White asked.

"Yeah." If that's where Duluth is.

Tom looked concerned. "Son, that's nearly two hundred miles from here."

"It is?" He paused only a second before he asked, "Is hitchhiking legal?"

Tom laughed. "That it is. Is he okay to go, Doc?"

Dr. White held up a sheet of paper in his hand and nodded. "The x-rays are normal. I really don't have a reason to keep him here."

"Then let me use the phone at the desk to check in with the station," Tom said. "Then I'll drive my friend here to the bus depo."

"But . . .?"

Tom was out the door before Ken could finish his question.

"He's a bossy ol' goat. But he has a good heart," Dr. White said, then turned to Ken with his hand extended. "Good luck to you. You can always reach me here at Memorial if you need to."

"Thanks for everything, Doctor." Ken shook the doctor's hand and walked out into the hall with him.

Tom scuffled up to them. "Divers found a jacket snagged to the car. Would it be yours?"

Ken recalled tugging his jacket off after it got caught in the wreck. "A brown tweed?" he asked.

"That's it!" Tom said. "Unfortunately, there was nothing in the pockets. Half the lining is tore off. Why don't we swing by the station and pick it up?"

"Look," Ken started to protest, but Tom grabbed him by the arm and said, "Let's get going" in a fatherly tone.

It was nearly noon by this time and even in the small city of Wausau, traffic was slow along what Tom called the main drag.

Ken could not fathom why, but everything looked *wrong*. Cars, buildings, people. The barrage of details dizzied him.

"Anything comin' to you, son? You're mighty quiet and those eyes of yours are as big as saucers."

"It's like-like I was just born, only I know I've seen this all before. But it feels so distant."

Tom pulled around to the back of a brick building and parked alongside other police vehicles. "I'll be right back." He paused and swung around to peer through the open window at him. "Now don't be thinkin' funny thoughts about taking off, or I'll come after you and arrest you for somethin'. I intend on taking you to the bus station and my wife says I *always* get my way."

The sergeant soon returned with the jacket. He tossed it at Ken. "It's dry, and a mite wrinkled but it might come in handy if a cool breeze comes up. With Duluth being a port city, nights can get cool up there, even this time of year."

The lining along the left side was ripped away, but otherwise the jacket appeared intact. Ken looked over at Tom. "Let me guess. Bus tickets in Wausau are free?"

Tom chuckled. "Whoever you are, you've a sense of humor." He pulled into a spot in front of the bus station under a sign that said, "Taxi's only." He pulled three tens out of his wallet and handed them to Ken.

"Look, Sergeant. I don't feel right—"

"Take it, son. Let's not waste time arguing; I've got to get back to work. Besides, if I stay here much longer, I might get a citation." The sergeant laughed silently and his belly shook.

Ken studied the older man. "Who chose you to be my guardian angel?"

Tom shrugged. "Friends have helped me out now and then. I believe in passing it on. Now get a move on or I'll give *you* a citation for loitering."

"You, sir, are mighty generous. I intend to mail you what I owe you as soon as I can." Though he had no idea when or how that could happen.

Ken got out of the car, came around to the driver's side, and extended his hand through the open window. "I'll never forget this Tom. . . at least, I don't think I will."

"Good luck, son." With a farewell wink the policeman backed the squad car up and drove off.

Ken went inside and purchased a one-way ticket to Duluth for $6.35. The older gentleman at the wicket, obviously more than a little deaf, informed the whole room of Ken's destination and the exact change. The bus would not leave for another two hours.

Ken sat down in the back row of benches and watched the comings and goings of people. Then fatigue seeped into him and he decided to take the lead from the older fellow in front of him and have a nap. Hopefully without the snoring or the drooling.

He wadded his wrinkled coat up and placed it behind his neck but the bench back was too short. He tried lying on his side with his head on the arm of the bench, but the lumps in his coat bugged him. He turned sideways on the bench, laid the coat out flat, and proceeded to roll it tightly.

Something crinkled. Something in the right lapel.

He studied the lining on the right flap. Nothing. He patted the lining. Nothing. He tried to fold the right side by itself. Nothing. But when he attempted to roll it, he *felt* something crinkle.

Adrenaline chased all remnants of fatigue away. There was something inside. Something that could provide answers.

Answers he was desperate for.

FIVE

Mauston, August 6, 1962

"What's wrong, Mom?"

Lou peered over the brim of her coffee cup at her son. Matt always seemed to know when something was bothering her.

"I got a call from Principal Wilson today. Mr. Stafford's twin brother has suffered a stroke and he's decided to retire and look after him."

"So?"

"So, the school is without a history teacher. With it being so close to the beginning of the school year and as hard as it is to attract teachers to a small town like Mauston, the rest of us will probably end up covering his class."

"So Mrs. Wilson had to cancel your art class?" Matt reached over and patted her arm.

She sighed and knew she would miss Matt's support when he left for West Point. Even through his teenage years, they had shared things that troubled them. They jokingly referred to their tete-a-tetes as pity parties.

"Only temporarily, I hope."

Matt took his breakfast dishes to the sink. "Would you like to see the portrait of Sandra?"

Lou jumped up. "Really? It's here?" Matt had been working on a portrait of his girlfriend for nearly three months now. Reluctant to have his mother see it prematurely, he had worked on it at Sandra's house.

Matt grinned at her. "I brought it home last night."

Lou playfully punched his shoulder. "Then how come you didn't show me last night?"

He chuckled. "I didn't want to wake you and have you all dopey and not able to critique properly."

He quickly stepped back to avoid another blow aimed in his direction and headed up the stairs. He looked more like his dad all the time, Lou thought. Matt was dark, whereas his dad had been blond, but he had his father's deep-set eyes and tall, muscular build. A lump formed in her throat and she stubbornly swallowed it. In eight days, Matt and his Uncle Steve would drive to New York State. Steve was a West Point Alumnus and Lou knew he was looking forward to showing off his nephew.

Matt pulled a sheet-wrapped rectangle from under his bed and carefully began to unwrap it.

"I hope that's one of my sheets. Else if Sandra's mom finds out she's likely to banish you forever."

He winked at her. "It's one of yours. Now turn your back while I get it ready."

She swung around impatiently. She couldn't explain the thrill that coursed through her whenever she looked at something new Matt had done. As if a small part of her came through his hands when they created.

"Okay!"

She turned back. He had angled it on his easel so it caught the light from the window. She inhaled quickly. This was good. She swallowed words that threatened to stumble out and walked over to study it so she could provide the detailed analysis he expected.

Sandra's essence oozed from the canvas as she straddled a chair. She propped her chin in one hand and draped her other arm loosely over the chair back. Her tentative smile hinted shyness while eagerness leaked out of her eyes. Wisps of hair escaped her ponytail and augmented her casual air.

Lou leaned closer to examine the strokes. They exhibited more control than she had seen in his previous oils. She took two steps back and forced herself to do one last general survey. Bottom line . . . it was a successful capture. She told him this before she virtually exploded with a tirade of details laced with the enthusiasm she had barely contained.

He awarded her one of his smiles, which she thought was the most beautiful in the world.

He proceeded to rewrap the painting. "Now, I can show Sandra."

"She hasn't seen it?"

"No, I wanted my critic to check it out first." Matt blushed, obviously pleased with her analysis.

A sad thought pierced her buoyancy. "Are you sure you don't want to take some of your art equipment with you to West Point?"

He sighed and glanced wistfully at his desk. "No. I'm not going to have any spare time there. My SATs barely cut the grade and I know I'll have to work my butt off just to keep my marks up. If it hadn't been for Uncle Steve, I doubt I'd have gotten in."

Lou's concern escaped in a sigh. She had exposed Matt to art at an early age, but he had preferred sports: football, soccer, anything moving – all to his Uncle Steve's pleasure. It had been a symbiotic relationship. While Steve adored his three daughters, Lou knew he had been thrilled to provide a manly presence for Matt's athletic endeavors. Steve had donated a share of his family's savings to help pay for Matt's tuition at West Point Military Academy, where Steve and his brother Ted had graduated.

Just prior to the beginning of their junior year, Matt had met Sandra, another art fanatic. He enrolled in art classes in order to spend more time with her. But soon, he developed a fetish of his own for charcoal sketching. Last year he had moved on to oils. Just after they received word he had been accepted into West Point, Matt confessed he'd harbored thoughts of applying for a fine arts degree at another university.

Steve had been blunt. What would Matt be able to do with a pansy-ass degree in fine arts when he could come out of West Point an officer in the armed forces with a valued degree? Lou's heart had torn at the hurt look in Matt's eyes.

Louise found it hard to deny her son anything. But she wanted him to get a good education and have a career, both of which seemed assured if he went to West Point.

Matt had relented and agreed to give the military academy a try. Steve was elated, but the look Matt sent Lou emphasized the word *try*.

From the look Matt now gave his art supplies she knew the last thing he wanted was to give up his art. She gave his shoulders a squeeze. He did not pull away.

"You have talent and can always return to painting whenever you want. What if you just took a few pencils and a sketchpad? It might prove to be therapeutic."

His deep laugh answered her. "No, it'll just make me want to do more. Besides, I won't be able to do it often enough and I'll just get disgusted. I have to practice, you know. I'm not a natural like someone else in the room."

Lou tousled Matt's thick dark hair. It was so long on top it was beginning to curl. He hadn't bothered to get a haircut, as he would be freshly shorn once he got to West Point.

He grinned at her. "Well, try to meet a man while I'm gone, will ya? You're too young and good looking to be spending Saturday nights alone."

Lou knew he would worry about her. Probably as much as she would about him. "And where in Mauston will I find one?" she teased.

"Good point. Maybe you should leave Mauston and go work in a large city. What's keeping you here, anyhow?"

"My job, for one. And Steve and Susan and the girls." After her accident Steve had used his influence as Juneau County Sheriff to get her a job teaching English at the public school in Mauston. After a career in New York, she had feared she would find the small town boring. But between her devotion to Matt and a burgeoning love of teaching, fulfillment found her. With Matt gone, would boredom return?

"I'm serious, Mom. I think it'd be good for you to leave here."

She gently cuffed his shoulder. "It's still home to you, mister. You'd better plan on frequent visits."

"If West Point ever lets us out of our cages," he said ruefully.

The phone rang and Matt sprinted down the steps. She heard him make plans for the evening. She sighed and looked about the room.

Too soon it would be way too tidy.

SIX

Wausau, August 6, 1962

As Ken entered the men's restroom of the bus station the pungent smell of inadequate and infrequent cleaning assaulted his nostrils. The latch in the first stall didn't work. The bolt in the second one was loose, but held.

With his back against the door he attempted to tear the lining of the jacket along the seam. The stitching proved hardy. For ten minutes he struggled to create an opening. Inwardly he reviewed his vocabulary of oaths. In spite of his memory loss, he was certainly able to remember a lot of bad words. Frustrated, he left the stall in search of something sharp.

On his way out Ken nearly collided with an older gentleman in a bow tie and wrinkled shirt. The man tipped his hat. "Try prune juice. Works for me!"

Ken swallowed a groan and continued his search. Short of breaking the mirror and risking seven years of worse luck, there was nothing with a sharp edge. He stepped outside the bus station and looked up and down the street. What would someone say if he walked up to him and asked for a sharp object? He decided against it for fear he would end up seeing Sergeant Tom again a lot sooner than either of them had expected.

There was an opening to his left. An alley. Twenty yards off the street a garbage bin stood sentinel. A quick search rewarded Ken with a shard of glass from a brown beer bottle. He wrapped his jacket around it and went back into the restroom. Once again inside the second stall, he operated on the lining. Finally he was able to make a slight tear in the fabric. Then he made a tear at right angles to the original rip.

Near the right shoulder a corner of what appeared to be a small document came into view. Could it be? Yes. It looked like a birth certificate encased in plastic. After more struggle, he was able to expose the full name: *Kenneth James O'Neil. DATE OF BIRTH: June 2, 1918. PLACE OF BIRTH: PITTSBURGH PA.*

He stared at it a long time. He mouthed the name silently and tried the taste of it on his tongue.

A crackle of static startled him. A woman's whiny voice announced the boarding of Bus 735 and listed a barrage of towns. The name *Mauston* sounded louder than the rest. Where the hell was Mauston? He folded his coat to hide the rips, draped it over his arm as a waiter would a towel, and headed out of the stall.

Once more his path crossed that of the old man he had seen earlier. The top of a brown paper bag protruded from the pocket of the old fellow's jacket, which explained his frequent visits to the restroom.

"You might try takin' a newspaper in with you!" the old man piped cheerfully.

Outside the washroom, indecision troubled Ken. Mauston or Duluth? Mauston had sounded louder and it felt louder.

Maybe he should follow his instinct. Maybe, by the time he got to Mauston, his memory would return.

With quickening steps that matched his pulse, he walked up to the wicket.

The nearly deaf man was still there.

Ken wondered where the woman with the whiny voice was.

"Can I get to Mauston from here?"

"Yep!" the teller yelled. "You have to take the 735 all the way down to Portage, then transfer to a bus that'll take you up to Mauston. But you'd better hurry. It's liable to pull out any minute now!" The other occupants of the bus station, and probably those in the buildings next door, were informed of the $1.35 change Ken received.

Ken managed to snag a seat to himself near the back of the bus. He tried to nap between stops, but his mind kept wandering. Kenneth O'Neil. Ken. The name failed to trigger any memories.

He squirmed in his seat. Fatigue and aching muscles made it hard to get comfortable. His neck threatened to go into spasm. After several stops, he had to endure a painful layover of two hours in Portage.

It was early evening by the time Ken stepped down onto the streets of Mauston. Signs at the edge of town had proven informative: Mauston was the seat of Juneau County. Population: 2,014. The Traditional County Fair would run August 11 to 19. To his disappointment, no more tidbits of memory came to him. Should he have gone to Duluth? Exhaustion augmented his self-doubt.

Ken walked up to the wicket. A young lady stopped chewing her gum to smile at him.

"Hello."

He tried to smile. "Would you please direct me to the nearest motel?" Yes, a shower and a few hours in a soft bed would work wonders.

"Yeah," she chewed for a second before she continued. "Back out near the highway there's a new one and a couple of old ones. The new one's probably nicer."

"How far is that?"

"Oh, let's see. Seven miles, or so."

"Is there anything closer?"

A few more chews, these more vigorous. "Let me see . . . well, there's one downtown, only that's a little expensive." She gave him the once over, then nodded as if she agreed with herself. She blew a bubble then quickly extinguished it with a snap. "How long you stayin'?"

Ken was taken aback by her boldness. "I'm not sure."

"Well, if you're going to be here awhile, you could check with Mrs. Lacey. Mr. Lacey passed away a year ago and I heard last Sunday in church that she's thinkin' of taking in boarders."

"Where does she live?"

"Half-way across town."

He suppressed a groan.

"Must be, what…" Another bubble here, this one swallowed whole. "Oh, about a mile."

One mile? He could walk that, couldn't he? Ken's tired body expressed doubts, but he ignored it.

She wrote down the address for him and pointed him in the general direction. Early in his journey his aches and pains returned to haunt him and his steps slowed. Then he smelled something . . . wonderful!

A turn at the next corner brought him within sight of a diner. It looked as if it had originally been a trailer. "Sandy's" shone in neon above the door.

Inside, he found himself the oldest person present. Teens crowded most of the booths, so he selected a stool at the counter.

A young man approached him and he looked to be the same age as the patrons. His freckled face smiled. "Can I help you, sir?"

"Yes. I'll have a . . ." Ken looked at the menu board above him. "Mmm, let's see, a hamburger, french-fries, and a vanilla milkshake."

"With the works?"

"Yes." Then Ken wondered what 'the works' meant.

A jukebox began to chime behind him and recognition smacked him as Elvis Presley belted out "Good Luck Charm." He actually remembered something. He was so happy he could have joined the teenagers on the small dance floor in front of the jukebox, but he was too tired.

The food was delicious and he had no trouble finishing the ample portion set in front of him. Someone put another coin in the jukebox and Gene Chandler sang "Duke of Earl." He was tempted to stay, listen to the music, and possibly eat something else, but decided he was too full.

The tab came to $2.75. That could not be right.

"Are you sure?" he asked the young man.

"Yes, sir. We raised our prices last week."

Ken then realized the lad assumed he thought he had been overcharged. He threw a five onto the table and headed to the restroom.

"Sir, your change!"

He looked back and gave the lad a grin. "That's yours."

The lad couldn't have smiled broader. "Thank you, sir!"

On the way to the restroom Ken reminded himself to be more cautious with the money the sergeant had given him. On the way out, another thought struck him. He once again approached the friendly lad behind the counter. "Do you know a Mrs. Lacey?"

"Yes, sir."

"How far is it to her place?"

"It oughtn't to take you more than twenty minutes. Turn left when you go out the door and go two blocks. Then cut through the schoolyard to Tremont Street. Walk till you come to the ballpark on your left and cut right across the baseball field. That'll put you onto Grove. You'll see an old grey house just on the left." He paused, then, "You a relative?"

"No. I'm hoping she'll rent me a room."

"I must warn you, she's a little weird. She and Mr. Lacey didn't like kids and on Halloween they used to scare away the little ones."

"Thanks for the warning and the directions."

Again the kid flashed him a row of white teeth. "Come again!"

I most likely will, Ken thought as he patted his happy belly.

Night had fallen, but the street lamps, though sparse, provided him with enough light to follow the young man's directions. Only the occasional honk from somewhere off to his right interrupted the peacefulness.

The length of the day wore on him and his legs grew heavy as he stepped onto the field. Each step became more difficult. The baseball diamond was not lit, and he stumbled over what he guessed to be the third-base bag but trudged on when he spotted the house.

As he got closer, the street lamps revealed more details. The lawn was unevenly cut and bald in spots where the sun had scorched it. One of the shutters on the upper level hung crookedly. The porch needed painting and its floor creaked under his feet as he crossed it. All the makings of a haunted house.

He had no watch, but guessed it to be past nine. The only light came from an upstairs window. He hoped Mrs. Lacey hadn't already gone to bed.

There was no doorbell, so he opened the screen door and rapped on the inside door. After waiting a few minutes, he knocked again.

"Hello? Mrs. Lacey?" he called.

No answer.

He rapped his knuckles against the window next to the door and hoped the different sound would alert the owner. There were no answering footfalls or other lights going on to indicate anyone had heard.

He went out onto the lawn and looked up at the window. "Mrs. Lacey?"

Still no response. Fatigue fed his frustration. The old lady probably wouldn't answer a door this time of night to someone she didn't know. What had he been thinking? Why the hell hadn't he thought to catch a cab to one of the motels while he was at the restaurant? He'd be in a soft bed by now.

The picture of dragging himself back to the diner depressed him. He started to turn away when he caught movement at the window above him. The curtains swayed in a slight breeze.

"Mrs. Lacey? I'm Ken O'Neil." The name came out easily enough although he still felt like a fraud. "I heard you were thinking of renting out a room."

A head framed in white appeared in the window. "Where did you hear that?"

Hope seeped into him. He gave as charming a smile as he could and prayed it didn't look fake. "A couple of places. At the bus station and at the diner."

"Which diner?"

"Sandy's."

"Never been there." She was quiet for so long, he feared she would chase him off.

"Mrs. Lacey?"

"Just a minute." The head disappeared. A minute later the porch light came on. She opened the inside door and studied him through the screen.

Cautiously he walked up the steps and across the porch.

"That's far enough."

He stopped a few feet shy of the door.

The crow's feet around her eyes multiplied. "You look too old to be dining at Sandy's. That place is for young folk."

Her scrutiny continued in silence. He was suddenly aware of how bad he must look. Wrinkled clothing. Stubble on his cheeks. No baggage.

"Where are you from?" She darted the question at him.

He thought a moment. "Originally, Pittsburgh. Today, I came from Wausau."

"On the bus?"

"Yes, Ma'am."

"I'm going to have to think about this. I only mentioned this renting business to the minister last Sunday. Lordy, you'd think people in this town would have more interesting things to talk about."

"I understand." At least he wanted to understand. But he was too tired to try and too tired to argue. He turned to leave.

"What did you say your name was?"

He turned back to her. "Kenneth O'Neil."

"What are you doing in Mauston?"

"Looking for work."

"What kinda work?"

He searched inwardly and felt a thrill of recognition. "I'm a teacher," he said then got excited by the certainty he felt.

"Of what?"

"History, among other things," he added in an attempt to sound as unsuspicious as possible. "Excuse, me, Ma'am. I'm awfully tired. Could I use your phone? I'd like to call a cab to go to a motel."

"Of course." Her quick affirmative surprised him. She unlatched the screen door and held it open for him.

"The phone's right there." She pointed to a small table at the bottom of the stairs. Beside it stood a double-armed chair draped in a knitted quilt. On the quilt sat a black cat. Goes along with the haunted house, Ken thought.

"Just dial zero and Bessie'll get you the number for Frank's cab."

Ken's legs wobbled. He had to sit. Without thinking, he picked up the plump cat and set it on his lap. Instead of fleeing as he had expected, the feline stretched once, then settled back down. He stared at the phone. It did not look right, but … he searched his memory, and, feeling Mrs. Lacey's eyes upon him, he picked up the top part. Yes, that was right. But where were the buttons? Only when the cat began to purr did he realize he was absently stroking it.

He tried to spin the round thing on the front, but it wouldn't turn. A gnarled hand reached over, stuck a finger in the last hole on the dial and dragged it around, turning the dial. It began to ring and as he waited, he risked a glance up, then wished he hadn't. Mrs. Lacey's pale eyes bore into his so sharply he felt she could see what a fake he was.

But instead of asking him to leave, she took the receiver from him and returned it to its cradle. "Do you drink tea?" she asked.

Too surprised to speak, he nodded.

"Come with me."

"Uh . . ." He pointed to the phone, but she ignored him and, still holding the cat, he followed her into the kitchen.

"Sit there." She pointed to one of two chairs at a small oval table.

After he sat down the cat immediately relaxed back into his lap. The warmth that exuded from its curled body was so relaxing Ken considered asking if he could sleep outside on the porch.

"Are you hungry, Mr. O'Neil?" she asked over her shoulder as she filled the kettle.

"No, thanks, ma'am. I ate at the diner."

"Just as well," she said. She returned to the table. "I don't cook much." She looked sharply at him as she said this. Her gaze dropped to the cat in his lap. "Looks as if Boots has taken a shine to you. First time she's ever done that, though I don't get many visitors. She used to sit in my husband's lap, just like that. You like cats?" Her eyes, of a color he had not yet determined, impaled him.

Did he? He looked at Boots whom he had continued to stroke without thinking. How the cat had acquired the moniker, he had no idea, for its paws were as black as the rest of it. The cat's loud purr made him want to close his eyes right then and there. He nodded.

"Hmmph." She took the whistling kettle off the burner and proceeded to make two cups of tea with one bag. She set a cup in front of him.

"Want some milk with that?"

"No, thank you."

"Sugar?"

"No, thanks." No more questions either, please. He just wanted to lie down.

She continued her scrutiny over the rim of her cup.

He took one sip of the weak tea then risked being rude by saying, "I'm sorry, Mrs. Lacey. I'm really tired. I'd better go call a cab."

"You could sleep in my husband's old room."

"Ma'am?" He wasn't sure he had heard correctly.

"Bed's clean. I made it up the day after he passed away. Lord knows why. Habit, I guess. You can sleep there tonight, if you wish. Boots will probably join you."

He was scared to blink in case she changed her mind.

She got up and took his nearly full cup along with hers to the sink. "Go along, now. It's to the right at the end of the hall. My room is on the left. Bathroom's at the end.

He set Boots on the floor and headed to the stairs. When he leaned on the railing, it wobbled so precariously he let go.

The mustiness of the room hit him when he entered. Perhaps he should have asked to sleep on the porch. He crossed over to a set of French doors that led out onto a balcony. When he opened them he was greeted with sweet summer air.

He returned to the bed and stretched out fully clothed on the patchwork quilt, nearly crushing Boots in the process. The cat circled once, then curled up against his side. Her ensuing warmth and gentle purr lulled him into a deep sleep.

SEVEN

Mauston, August 14, 1962

Sheriff Steve Jensen let out the clutch as he turned the corner. The station wagon didn't have the pedal or the maneuverability of his county-issued vehicle, but it should get his nephew Matt and him to West Point, no problem.

His wife Susan had fallen in love with the wagon five years before when they shopped for a new vehicle that could accommodate their two daughters and the one on the way. "And it would be great for groceries," she had added. He had wanted to argue that his pick-up would do fine for groceries but it sure didn't suit a family of five. So he had agreed to the wagon. Today it would come in handy to move Matt's stuff to West Point.

He hammered on the horn twice to let Matt know he had arrived. He climbed out and allowed himself a lengthy stretch as he gave the exterior of the house the once over. Come next spring, it would need a new coat of paint. He shook his head and grinned as he remembered how Lou had insisted she do some of the work herself just after she had purchased the home. She used her splinted hand as a hook around a ladder rung while she leaned over and scraped at the old paint with her left hand. That lady was one stubborn customer and unfortunately it looked as if Matt took after her in that respect.

When Steve's younger brother Ted was killed in Korea, Steve had wanted Lou and her young son to move to Mauston right away, where Steve could lend a helping hand now and then. But no, she wanted to be independent and raise her son in New York. He had wondered how she would be able to support them on the inconsistent earnings of an artist. Only after she lost the use of her right hand in a car accident did she allow Steve to help.

After nearly a year of expensive rehabilitation, Lou agreed to move to Mauston and accept a teacher's position. In the seven years since, they had become close friends and Lou was now like a sister to both him and Susan.

Matt came out the front door, a bulging duffel bag slung over his back. Steve swallowed an unexpected lump that rose in his throat. Except for his dark hair, Matt looked more and more like a younger version of Ted. Steve and his brother had only been thirteen months apart in age, and they had grown up on their farm in rural Kansas the best of friends. Steve still missed him.

Lou followed her son down the steps. Perched atop her splinted hand was a cardboard box. In her left she carried a picnic basket. Steve hurried to take some of her load.

"We should be at West Point by tomorrow evening," he said. "I suppose you packed us enough food to last a week."

Lou smiled at him. "Not the way my son eats. He eats almost as much as his uncle now."

"Now be nice." Steve said. He patted his thickening waist after he set the food in the back behind the duffel bag. "Between your cooking and Susan's, a fellow doesn't stand much of a chance."

"Just remember," Matt said, "half of that food has my name on it."

Lou gave them each a kiss on the cheek. "Now drive carefully. And call me when you get to West Point." To Steve she added, "And don't tell him any more stories about you and his father. I don't want him to get any ideas."

Steve grinned. "No promises." He and his brother had enjoyed their adolescence. Their father used to refer to it as 'being wild.' After a near scrape with the law, Hank Jensen had pulled a favor and gotten both his sons registered at West Point. The academy soon split the brothers up. Ted became a naval cadet; Steve was ushered into the army.

"Can I drive?" Matt asked the moment they rounded the first corner.

"Just as soon as we hit the edge of town." Lou knew Matt would be driving part of the way. Steve just figured it would lessen her worry if he were the one to drive off. Once on the highway, Steve pulled over and walked around to the passenger side while Matt shuffled across the seat.

Steve slammed his door shut and grinned at his nephew. "Let's hit the road!" He was excited about Matt going to West Point. Matt was a smart fellow. After all, he must have some of his uncle's genes. Steve had often felt Matt hadn't tapped his full potential, be it sports or academics.

Well, the military academy would soon cure that, he thought. Hell, Ted and Steve had been just youngsters fooling around until they entered West Point. There, they grew into responsible adults.

Before leaving for Korea, they had made a pact. If one of them didn't make it back, the other would look after their family. Steve was in open combat with the infantry division. He should have been the one to die. Not Ted, who was in naval communications. Five weeks before a ceasefire was established, Ted died when his ship went down in a storm off the coast of Korea.

Steve had been devastated. He accepted an honorable discharge and moved in with Susan's parents who ran a farm north of Mauston. Three years later he successfully ran for the position of Juneau County Sheriff. He never regretted the decision. He was content with his job and his extended family. All was good. And all would be good for Matt.

He grinned over at his nephew but the solemn look on the lad's face told him that Matt did not share his enthusiasm.

* * *

Ken tried the right hand side of the double doors of the school. It was locked. He tried the other side. That was locked, too. He looked at his new Timex. Eight forty-five. He was early. Mrs. Lacey had offered him the use of the Mr. Lacey's 1952 Buick Riviera, which, since Mr. Lacey's demise, had only collected dust in the garage at the back of her property. Ken had declined, as he somehow *knew* he did not know how to drive a car. How he knew this he didn't know. As it turned out, the school was only a fifteen-minute walk from Mrs. Lacey's house.

Out of the pocket of a borrowed suit coat of the late Mr. Lacey, he pulled out the ad from yesterday's paper that Mrs. Lacey had cut out for him.

Required immediately: History teacher for Mauston Public School. Submit resume to Principal Irma Wilson, P.O. Box 257, Mauston, Wisconsin. Call 6748 to set time for an interview.

Instead of calling, he figured his chances might increase if he came in person. He replaced the paper and noticed the angry calluses on his palms.

He had spent much of the past eight days repairing the porch and shutters. Painting was next on the agenda. Then he would tackle the yard. So far, Mrs. Lacey had refused to collect rent. But she hadn't objected to the repairs he had done. And he had learned something else about himself: he enjoyed the work.

Mrs. Lacey stayed mostly in her room and tapped away at her typewriter, often at odd hours. He didn't ask her what she was working on, as he had been grateful she had kept her questions to a minimum. His memory hadn't returned, but he sensed he was doing the right thing.

And applying for this teaching job was the right thing, too, he felt. Even more so because what money Sergeant Tom had given him was just about gone. Ken had called Tom and said he would return the thirty dollars as soon as he earned a paycheck. The call had proven helpful, as Tom then suggested Ken use him for a reference.

Ken turned around at the sound of footsteps on the stairs behind him. A big, solid woman walked up to him. She appeared to be in her mid-fifties. Her confident step and demeanor warranted respect.

"May I help you?" she asked in a deep voice.

Soldiers would march to that tone, he thought. He held out his hand.

"Principal Wilson? I'm Ken O'Neil."

She shook his hand. "You're the gentleman fixing up the Lacey place."

He nodded.

"What can I do for you, Mr. O'Neil?"

"I would like to apply for the teaching position that's open."

"The history teacher's position?"

"Yes." He swallowed past his constricting throat and attempted what he hoped came across as a warm smile. "I really need this job, Mrs. Wilson."

She looked him over. "Well, you deserve points for eagerness. Come on in and let's chat."

She pulled a huge ring of keys out of her purse and opened the door. The smell of recently applied floor wax filled the empty hallway. Ken followed Mrs. Wilson as she turned the first corner and unlocked another door into an inner office. She clicked a switch and the dark office cast off some of its gloom. The orderly desktop perpetuated a no-nonsense atmosphere.

Dust wouldn't have a chance to settle here, he thought.

"Have a seat, Mr. O'Neil." She pointed to a chair across from her. A chair no doubt reserved for some poor student called in for bad behavior. "Tell me about yourself."

He froze. What the hell could he tell her? He began in what he hoped sounded like a normal tone. "I'm from Pittsburgh. I . . ." He paused. How could he ever have hoped to get this job?

She watched him closely and he knew this woman would not be easily fooled. "You have taught before," she prompted.

"I have," he answered, relieved at the truth he felt in his answer.

"What grades?"

At that moment, he decided he had no choice but to be truthful. He told her about the accident and his subsequent amnesia. "I don't know how I know this, but I am certain I have taught history. I can't remember anything else, though. What grades or where." When he finished, he leaned back and waited for her to point to the door.

She stared at him a moment, then said. "That story is too strange not to be true. Now tell me why I should hire you."

He thought about this a minute. "I know I can teach history, Mrs. Wilson. I know I can do a good job. What I don't know is how I know that."

She shook her head. "I'm sorry Mr. O'Neil. As badly as we need a teacher, I can't just hire someone into the position with no credentials, no references."

"I can give you one reference."

"Oh?"

His guardian angel. "Sergeant Tom Stevens of the Wausau Police Department."

She nodded. "Well, I'll have to follow up on this and I've got a full slate for the next couple of days. Will you be staying at Mrs. Lacey's?"

He nodded and rose. "I appreciate whatever time you can give me."

"No promises, Mr. O'Neil. But I will let you know, one way or another."

As he walked home any hope he had was replaced with increasing despondency. What had he been thinking? How could he have hoped to get that job?

Once he heard back from her that the answer was no, he'd try to get a job somewhere else. He needed a job if he was going to stay in Mauston.

And something told him he needed to be here.

EIGHT

Mauston, August 27, 1962.

Ken opened his eyes and blinked. He pulled himself out of bed and groggily approached the open French doors. Beyond the balcony lay a green yard awash in morning sunshine. Such a beautiful day. So why did he feel so worried? What was it that he had to do?

He could travel to Pittsburgh and research records to see if he could learn who his parents had been or if he had any other relatives. But he couldn't do that until he found work and earned money.

He walked out onto the newly boarded balcony. He remembered the weatherman on the local radio station had promised temperatures would reach higher than normal. He looked at his watch: seven-fifty-five. He'd better get moving if he wanted to get the back of the house scraped before it got too hot.

He borrowed Mrs. Lacey's radio from the kitchen and worked to the beat of the music. He finished scraping and began to sweep up shavings that had fallen onto the deck. He felt good while he worked. Physically and mentally.

The music helped connect him to reality. Neil Sedaka's "Breaking Up Is Hard To Do" got him swinging to the beat and using his broom as a dance partner. Then Dion followed and the broom became a microphone as he sang along: "Well, I'm the type of guy who'll never settle down——." He froze in mid-sentence.

Principal Wilson stared at him from the edge of the deck. But even embarrassing himself could not dampen his mood. He shut the radio off, bowed low, and greeted her with a cheerful, "Good Morning, Principal Wilson."

She nodded. "I believe it is. I see now why you didn't hear me knock. Would Mrs. Lacey be in?"

He hid his disappointment it was not him she had come to visit. "Yes, she's up in her room. Do you want me to fetch her?"

"Yes, please. Tell her I'll wait for her on the front porch."

He bounded up the stairs and knocked on Mrs. Lacey's door. The tapping stopped. She opened the door only a crack. He had never seen the inside of her room.

"Mrs. Wilson is downstairs on the front porch. She would like to have a word with you."

He followed her down the steps and outside to offer the ladies something to drink. Mrs. Lacey beat him to it.

"Hello, Irma. Would you like some iced tea?" Before Mrs. Wilson could respond, Mrs. Lacey turned back to Ken. "Would you be a dear and fetch us some?"

"Of course." He retreated to the kitchen. Mrs. Lacey had allowed him to play maid. The house smelled fresher and the sun shone brightly through washed glass and opened curtains. They had developed a routine where he cooked breakfast and supper. Lunch was achieved individually.

He searched the cupboards for a tray, found one, and washed the dust off it. Mrs. Lacey was not one for homemaking. From what he had been able to determine, the lady spent all day in her room either at the typewriter or reading the ten or more newspapers from around the country that she had delivered daily to the house.

The minister and his wife had brought a tin of muffins over the day before and Ken placed two of these on the tray along with two tall tumblers of iced tea. Feeling like a butler, he took the tray out to the porch.

"Why, thank you, Kenneth." Mrs. Lacey said.

Ken sensed he was not to be included in their conversation so he exited. He returned to the back porch, turned up the radio, and proceeded to sweep the deck without performing.

A few minutes later he felt a light tap on his shoulder. He turned around to see Mrs. Lacey smiling at him. She seemed happier these days and he knew her elevated spirits contributed to his improved mood.

"She wants to talk to you." Without another word Mrs. Lacey turned and went up the stairs. By the time Ken reached the front porch he could hear the typewriter keys dancing again.

Mrs. Wilson pointed to a wicker chair across from her. "Have a seat, Mr. O'Neil." Her expression remained stern and he wondered if she was capable of looking sad or happy. She fixed him with her hazel eyes. When she allowed herself a short sigh, he feared the worst.

"I am in a rather difficult position, Mr. O'Neil. No one else has applied for the position and the school term begins a week from today." Her short pause allowed him to initiate optimism. "I have talked to Sergeant Stevens and it appears you convinced him you are a good person."

But I haven't convinced you, have I? Ken thought.

"Also, Mrs. Lacey has lived in Mauston a long time and I value her opinion. It appears you have made a fan of her as well." She looked at the new, yet unpainted boards beneath her feet. "I am certain she appreciates your help." The eyes returned to lock onto his. "If I am to offer you a position, it must be under certain non-negotiable terms."

He smiled at her. "You have the advantage here, Mrs. Wilson. And I need a job."

"I am prepared to give you the position temporarily. If another teacher with proper accreditation applies, or if you fail to meet required standards, I will not hesitate to release you without a moment's notice. I plan to attend your classes on a regular basis and your students will be asked about your teaching, both content and style. Do you find this acceptable?"

"Yes, ma'am." He could not help but smile at her.

"Well, then." She stood up and smoothed her skirt, which didn't need smoothing, as this was not a lady who wrinkled easily. "I expect you to report at eight o'clock on Wednesday morning for orientation with Mrs. Morse. This will take most of the morning. She will give you the curriculum information and the necessary texts. By ten o'clock Thursday morning I want to see your outline of the classes for the first semester. We will review it in my office. A staff meeting will be held that afternoon at one o'clock. Classes resume the following Tuesday at eight a.m."

Ken grinned again and held out his hand. "I really appreciate this opportunity, Principal Wilson."

She shook his hand as firmly as a longshoreman. One eyebrow arched. "Let's just hope you can teach as well as you make iced tea."

She did not smile, but he noted a softening about her eyes before she brusquely left and marched up the street.

He wanted to shout and kick up his heels but Mrs. Wilson was still within range to see and hear him, so instead he went into the house. Mrs. Lacey met him at the bottom of the steps, her arms laden with newspapers.

He reached for them. "Here, let me take those."

She handed them over. It was a heavy load and he wondered how she had managed to bring it down the stairs.

"Just put them by the back door," she said. "Jeb picks them up for me every Tuesday and takes them to the dump."

Dump? Not recycled? He said nothing and added the stack to the already sizable one by the back door. A heading on the top page caught his eye. It was the *New York Times* from three days before. "FALLOUT SHELTERS RECOMMENDED OVER EVACUATION." It contained a front-page article on a civil defense plan for the likelihood of nuclear attack.

Nuclear Attack. The phrase bounced in his head. Nausea gripped his stomach as his head flooded with images, horrible ones of bodies roasted to blackened bones. Whole cities reduced to rubble.

There was something he had to do. What? he screamed inwardly. He looked about the yard, down at the deck, up at the sky, the trees, and finally back to the newspaper in front of him. There was no answer there and no answer inside him.

NINE

Mauston, August 29, 1962

Lou surveyed the room: the glossy emptiness of her desktop, the rich green of freshly washed blackboard, and the perfect alignment of the rows of desks. She knew it wouldn't take long for students to restore it to the more normal state of disarray.

"Hello, there, Louise!"

Lou knew who it was before she looked up. There were two people employed at the school who did not call her 'Lou' when students weren't around. Principal Wilson, who used everyone's surname and Alice Morse, who, for some reason, had trouble using the shortened version. That and a fetish for gossip were the woman's only weaknesses in Lou's opinion.

Alice was the glue that held the school together amid the normal realm of chaos. Her official title was receptionist, but she did more than answer the phone. She ordered supplies, always knew where things were, or where things could be fixed. She scheduled the PTA meetings, staff meetings, and organized the staff functions. All of this with efficiency and a bubbling affect. She was in her late fifties and Lou hoped the woman would not retire until after Lou quit teaching.

"Welcome back, Alice. Did you have a nice summer?"

"Yes indeed! Did you meet the new history teacher?"

"No, but Mrs. Wilson made my day when she called last week and told me she had filled the position. Now I get to teach art along with literature."

"I met him this morning. Oooh, what a charmer!"

"Really?" This did not fit the description of the history teachers Lou had met in the past.

"He's got these deep dark eyes that look at you like you are the only person on the planet. And he's so suave." She spread her hand along an imaginary tabletop. 'Smoo-ooth!"

"Does Mr. Morse have anything to worry about here?" Lou teased.

"Heavens no! Ken O'Neil is too young for me – though he doesn't look much older than you . . ."

"Now hold on. Don't go playing cupid. The last thing I need is a man in my life." It had been a couple of years since Lou had dated and she did not intend to put herself through *that* again.

"If you were wise, you'd reserve your decision until after you meet him. This fellow has an elegant, big city feel about him. Classy. He'll really dress up our staff room."

Lou laughed. The staff room could use a little dressing up. The only other males were Jim Cage and George Miller. Jim, a tall, overweight fellow in his late thirties, taught geography and coached football. George, who was at least sixty-five - though no one knew that for sure - taught mathematics. He was thin, wiry, and appeared shorter because of his curved spine. Behind his spectacles resided a brilliant mind. The rest of the teachers were women ranging in ages from twenty-four to sixty and all married except for Lou.

"I'm too busy and too mature for romance, Alice, so go buy yourself some paperbacks." Lou's stern look only bounced off Alice's cheery expression. "Has Jim finished with the Gestetner?"

"I believe the copier's free. See you later!" With a naughty smile, Alice carried her plump form through the door.

Lou then realized why her desk had looked so clutter free. She had neglected to bring the handout she had prepared for the first day of school. She could ride home and get it or bring it the next day. Since the copier was sure to be busier the following day, she decided go back to her house, have a bite to eat, then return with the handout.

She hadn't driven a vehicle since her accident and now her main mode of transportation was her trusty bicycle. A one-way trip took twelve to fifteen minutes. When the weather was inclement, she took the bus or, if in a rush, a taxi.

At the end of her lunch hour, she arrived back at the school with her handout. She parked her bicycle in the stalls. When she was halfway up the steps she saw Mrs. Wilson hold the door open for a man loaded down with folders and textbooks.

The new history teacher. He concentrated on his load and did not look up until he was beside her. He started to smile, then froze. His arms shuffled the sliding books in an attempt to keep his load from toppling.

"Hello," Lou said as she passed him and wondered if she had mayonnaise on her nose or something worse. If he had stared at her hand, she would have understood his reaction. But it was her face he had reacted to.

She continued up the steps and turned around at the top to find him still watching her. His dark eyes met hers only briefly before he turned away. He missed the next step and his load tumbled forward. While trying to recover them he missed another step and the entire bundle tumbled out of his arms.

He then piled everything on the ground in front of him and studied the books intensely, as if waiting for them to take flight.

Lou realized Mrs. Wilson still held the door open behind her. "Our new history teacher," she said in her no-nonsense tone. "I hope he will have less difficulty juggling the curriculum."

Lou grinned and followed Mrs. Wilson inside.

Alice pounced on Lou when she entered the outer office. "Mr. O'Neil just left. Did you see him?"

Lou only nodded and headed into the copy room. Alice's description of O'Neil didn't match the man she had just seen. He had looked pretty jittery for someone who was supposed to be 'smoo-ooth.'

* * *

Somehow, despite the image of the woman's face flashing in his head, Ken managed to make it back to Mrs. Lacey's. He walked up the stairs, past the *tapatapatap* and went into his room. He set the books down on the bed then collapsed beside them.

He looked at his hands. They were trembling. His heart danced to a double time beat. He was sure he had *known* that woman and had hoped it was a sign his memory was returning. He studied the imprint in his mind. It reminded him of when he had first seen his own face in a mirror. Familiar, but not quite right.

He sighed. Things had just begun to seem normal when, once more, his sanity felt threatened. Maybe he should get himself committed instead of trying to resume a normal life. What on earth had Mrs. Wilson seen in him when she hired him to teach children? Was he doing the right thing teaching these kids?

A feeling that he was calmed him and he decided to do what he had done for the past three weeks: Go with his gut feeling and try to be a good citizen.

He looked up and saw Mrs. Lacey in the doorway. Her pale eyes assessed him. Was she going to tell him to leave?

But she surprised him by asking, "What's it like to drown?"

"What?"

"What's it like to drown?"

How much did she know about him? Perhaps more than he did. "How should I know?"

"You nearly drowned, up in Wausau."

He walked over to her. "How do you know this?"

Her innocent smile grew wider. "I read newspapers, you know."

"Was there an article about me?"

She nodded.

"What did it say?"

She tapped a bony, wrinkled index finger on his chest. "They called you a hero."

He shook his head. "I didn't save anyone. Did it talk about my amnesia?"

She nodded.

"When did you figure out I was the person who nearly drowned?"

"Shortly after you came."

"How did you do that?" Mauston was a long way from Wausau, both geographically and figuratively.

She turned to head down the stairs. "I can add two and two and come up with four, you know. Come down and have some lunch. I've more questions for you."

He eagerly followed her. Maybe her questions would result in answers he was looking for. He allowed her to make the ham sandwiches, although he would have enjoyed them more with mustard and lettuce. And more ham.

"So you let me stay here, even when you knew I couldn't remember who I was, or what I was doing here?"

She smiled at him and pointed to a chair. "Sit." She poured them each a glass of milk and sat down. She took a bite of sandwich, a swallow of milk, then waved her arm and said. "Look around you. Both the house and myself have benefited from you living here. Besides, Boots liked you, so I knew you were a good person." She took another bite and swallowed. "So tell me exactly what you remember from your drowning."

"Why do you want to know?"

The sun was on the other side of the house and the kitchen was in shadow, so he couldn't be certain, but she appeared to blush at his question.

"Research," she finally said.

"Ah. You writing a novel or something?"

She nodded shyly, then repeated her request.

He thought back and gave her what details he could remember.

"So, no white light or tunnel or anything like that?"

He shook his head.

"What about floating above your body?"

"No." He pulled at his memory. "But I do remember a hand reaching for me – it must have been Sergeant Stevens. Sorry, I'm not much help."

She waved at him in dismissal. "No worries. I'm just glad you survived."

Ken wished he could remember more. As if knowing he needed comforting, Boots rubbed against his shins under the table. He reached down to pet her. "Why do you call your cat Boots?"

Mrs. Lacey chuckled as she took her plate and glass to the sink. "We had just gotten her. She was so tiny and loved to curl up in dark places. We couldn't find her once and got real worried. We figured she was gone until the next morning when my husband went to pull on his overshoes. She was fast asleep in one of them. So, 'Boots' it was."

When Mrs. Lacey returned to her room, Ken washed the few dishes. His earlier frustration mellowed when he realized that to this woman, his past was unimportant. She accepted him as he was.

For the first time since waking up in Memorial Hospital, he felt a little less alone.

TEN

Mauston, August 30, 1962

Lou glanced at her watch and whispered a curse. She was still two blocks from the school and the meeting had started fifteen minutes ago. Principal Wilson waited for no one. Another curse flew at her disabled bike. Halfway to the school she had blown a tire. By the time she shoved the bike between the rails, she was perspiring and flustered.

She endured Mrs. Wilson's stern look, ignored Jim Cage's smirk, and proceeded directly to the last empty chair in the room. No doubt she would hear additional taunts about her mode of transportation before the day was out.

It wasn't until after she sat down that she noticed Ken O'Neil three seats to her left. He gave her a brief unreadable look then returned his attention to the principal. His tweed jacket, starched shirt and tie added to his aura of freshness and alertness. His gaze returned to her and with a start she realized Mrs. Wilson was talking about her.

" . . . Art classes. Included is a schedule of the examination dates for each semester, general assemblies, PTA meetings and workshops. Please study it carefully and get back to me immediately if you notice any conflicts."

After reviewing the minutes of the last school board meeting, Mrs. Wilson handed the chair over to Alice, who quickly detailed the contents of the bulletin board at the back and emphasized the sign-up lists for PTA meetings, dances, and school clubs.

On more than one occasion Lou caught O'Neil studying her. She returned his look directly and hoped her gaze proved as impenetrable as his. At the conclusion of the meeting she followed Mrs. Wilson out.

"I had a flat tire," she said when she managed to catch up to the quickly moving woman.

Mrs. Wilson paused and turned to her. "May I give you a lift home?" Her stern look hadn't altered, but Lou knew the question signaled her tardiness had been forgiven.

"No, thanks. I want to set up my art supplies. Alice says they arrived this morning. Besides, I'll stop at Gus's garage on my way home and get the tire fixed."

"See you tomorrow, then." Mrs. Wilson resumed her efficient pace.

Lou lugged two boxes of supplies from the storeroom to her classroom. She opened them in what she had decided would be 'the art corner.'

She returned to the storeroom for the last of the supplies. Onto the reverse side of a canvas, she placed several small items: boxes of brushes, erasers, sketching pencils. She paused at the door of her room when she saw O'Neil crossing the hall to the Coca-Cola machine.

He studied it a minute before saying to no one in particular, "What, no diet?"

Diet? Unless the suit coat hid bulges, the man didn't appear to have a weight problem.

He didn't notice her so she allowed herself to linger. He pulled a coin out of his pocket, dropped it in the slot, and then pushed on the front of the machine with his fingertips, as if he expected that to do something. When he kept trying this, she gave in to her curiosity and approached him. He glanced at her just long enough for her to see his frown of frustration.

She shifted her load onto her splinted arm, opened the narrow glass door, pulled out a bottle from its slot, and handed it to him.

"Oh . . . uh thanks." He studied the bottle, "Cool!"

"Did you expect the soda to be warm?" Lou asked.

A puzzled frown again creased his forehead, then disappeared when he smiled. He twisted his palm over the pop cap. It wasn't until he yelped that she realized he had attempted to open it with his hand. He then gripped the cap carefully with his fingertips and tried to twist it off.

"No, silly." She took the bottle from him. He watched in silence as she used the opener on the machine to pry the cap off. She handed the opened bottle back to him.

"Oh, right." He looked a little embarrassed. "Thanks," he saluted her with the bottle. "Would you like one?"

In an attempt to hide her splinted hand she folded both forearms under her load. "No, thanks."

Her camouflage failed. He pointed to her right arm. "How did that happen?"

She swallowed the lump created by his bluntness. This virtual stranger had asked about her injured hand as casually as if he had asked about her flat tire. She hoped he would retract the question when she hesitated, but no, he stood there waiting for an answer, and looked at her with those soul-searching eyes Alice had talked about.

Her first response was to flee, but a resolve came over her. She could be equally as forthright. "I was in a car accident and nearly had my arm amputated. I can't lift my hand without the brace on."

She expected him to flinch. At the very least, display pity.

But his expression only softened slightly when he asked, "Does it hurt?"

"Only on rainy nights." She went on the offensive. "How's your hand?"

He grinned as he raised his scratched palm. "It's okay."

"Do you always try to open bottles that way?"

Instead of answering, he stepped a little closer and asked, "Does your presence always make fellows degenerate into mindless oafs?"

She smiled at his offer of the upper rung of the teasing ladder. "No. You're the only one."

He shrugged shyly, and then responded, "Well, maybe the others just aren't as perceptive as I am."

She blinked at the unusual, yet flattering compliment. She had heard so few in recent years that an unwanted blush crept into her cheeks. She turned to leave and collided with Mrs. Wilson. The canvas hit the floor, boxes split open, and pencils and brushes escaped in different directions. Ken stooped with her to help her pick them up.

Mrs. Wilson spoke over their heads. "Well, some of the staff appear to be developing clumsiness. I wonder if it's a virus of some sort."

Ken's face was close to Lou's, and when she looked up, the mirth in his eyes made her giggle.

As Mrs. Wilson walked off they heard her say, "I do hope it's contagious," to which they both laughed.

After he helped Lou carry the supplies into her room, he said, "Have a good evening." Then with a salute of his soda, he left.

She sat in her chair and relived the scene. She touched her cheeks. A faint warmth persisted. This strange man had made her feel attractive. After openly discussing her right hand. She looked at her brace.

For the first time in eight years it did not look so ugly.

* * *

Bejing, April 7, 2049

Ko pulled the white T-shirt over the bruises and welts that decorated his torso. Shimira had stolen into his room the night before. It would be their last time together. At least until he returned to the present.

He donned the denim jacket and studied his reflection in the mirror. His casual dress had been chosen to make his presence less noticeable in 1962.

His short haircut made his mixed-race features appear similar to those of a Native American. This and his perfect English and exemplary record had swayed the votes of the council in his selection for this mission.

The door opened behind him. A soldier saluted. It was time.

Without a word they traversed the long, bare hallway to the elevator. He knew by the length of the trip down that he had never before been this far beneath the surface of the earth. The smooth whir of the elevator diminished as it slowed to a halt.

Two men in white lab coats sprinted past the open elevator door. Ko could not discern individual words from the faint babble of excitement in the distance but it was obvious something was wrong.

Another uniformed man planted himself in front of Ko and saluted.

"Please return to the surface, sir."

Ko rode back up to the waiting room he had just vacated. He sat down at the desk and initiated the retinal scan. The desktop slid open and a thin screen flipped to the vertical position. He opened the file on the Nuclear Conflict of '62 and clicked on   O'Neil's article that had been published in 2041.

It was difficult to comprehend how the most advanced nation at the time could have made such a mistake. On October 25th, 1962, a mechanical failure in an alarm at an American airfield had led to friendly fire over the Atlantic, which in turn prompted both the United States and the Soviet Union into thinking the other had pre-empted.

Equally unbelievable was the fact that just thirty-five years after quantum teleportation had been achieved, New America had managed to conquer time travel, thanks to the defection of scientist Ito Nishimura. That they would tamper with time without knowing what repercussions would occur proved just how careless American thinking could be.

An hour and a half later the door opened and the First Minister entered. Ko, deeply honored, stood up and bowed. The minister waved for him to sit down and chose a chair opposite Ko.

"We have suffered a setback." The minister spoke to him in Phyong'yang, Ko's native Korean dialect. Another honor.

Ko revealed none of the optimism that blossomed within him. A setback meant delay, not cancellation. And perhaps another opportunity to see Shimira.

"There was an error in the calculation of the positive energy densities of the materials used in the primary chamber and, on initiation, minor warping occurred."

Ko nodded. He did not understand the physics involved and he suspected the minister only relayed information given to him.

"The scientists cannot agree on the time needed to repair the unit. The more optimistic ones predict a matter of weeks. But we still have time. As long as you arrive before October 25th, you will be able to stop him from changing history."

After mutual bows, the minister left.

Ko sighed at the thought of more waiting.

But a few more weeks in 2049 would not change what was going to happen in 1962.

ELEVEN

Mauston, October 15, 1962

Lou looked at her watch. Ten past four. The staff meeting would start at promptly four-fifteen regardless of who was present. But most of the teachers were already there. Ken entered the room and promptly began to cough. He waved at the smoky haze. With a grimace he forced the window open as far as it would go.

With more waving and hacking, he exclaimed, "Whew! The students don't have to sneak a cigarette in the bathroom, they could just come in here and inhale."

"Oh, does the smoke bother you, Kenny?" Jim's throat sounded tight. Then he exhaled in a deliberately slow fashion and aimed his pollution directly at Ken.

"Oh, no." Ken coughed again. "I just hate to see the students waste precious money on cigarettes when they could develop lung cancer right here without spending a cent." Ken paused as if looking for a laugh, but he received only puzzled frowns. He sat down beside Lou and deflected her puzzled look with a charming smile that tickled her on the inside.

Other than Ken, Lou and Alice were the only ones not smoking. To save money Lou had quit smoking after Ted died, except for the occasional one with Steve after Sunday dinner.

Principal Wilson entered the room. Lou could tell by her voice that she was pleased the meeting would begin two minutes early. Mrs. Wilson's normally stern countenance softened slightly at the conclusion of the meeting and Lou had to admit this had been the smoothest first six weeks she could remember in her seven years at the school. And the most stimulating. She thoroughly enjoyed teaching art and she wondered why she hadn't done it before.

She left the building the moment the meeting closed. A gentle breeze caressed her face as she headed down the cement stairs. Its warmth promised at least a few more days of Indian summer.

As she pulled her bike clear of the rack she noticed the rear tire was once again completely flat. Gus had warned her his repair had been only temporary. It looked as if she would have to spring for a new tire.

"Can I help?"

She turned as Ken stepped toward her. His dark eyes were warm with concern.

"No, thanks. Another flat is all. It's a nice day to walk home, anyway."

"Do you have far to go?"

"Not really, the garage is just the other side of Main Street."

"May I push your bike for you?"

She hesitated only a second but that was all he needed to take hold of the handlebars. He pushed the bike along and they soon fell into an easy pace.

She wondered why she felt so comfortable with him. Especially considering his reaction the first time he had seen her. The rumor mill at the school hinted at a mysterious past, of which only Mrs. Wilson was privy. And Ken himself had shared very little with any of the other teachers. All anyone seemed to know was that he was from Pittsburgh.

She realized she wanted to know if there was someone else in his life. "What brought you to Mauston, Ken?"

"Work."

"Why here? Mauston is so small."

He shrugged again. "I'm not sure."

She stopped and faced him. "That's a weird answer."

Muscular shoulders moved inside his cotton shirt as he shrugged. "It's the truth." He proceeded to move along.

"In a small town, people usually know everything about everybody. But even after the two months you've been here, we know nothing about you."

"I suppose I should tell you what I know since you're letting me walk you home," he said.

Another strange response. She decided it would be best if she knew more before she let her attraction grow. "Yes, you should."

The story he told created more questions. The near drowning. The amnesia. Lou's loneliness paled in comparison with what he must be experiencing.

"Have you started to remember anything?" she asked.

He shook his head. "Not much."

She decided to be brazen. After all, he was the first man she had felt attracted to in a long time. "So you could be married?"

Again he shook his head. "No."

She wanted to ask him how he could be so certain, but the sadness in his tone prompted her to end her inquisition.

Within minutes they reached Gus's garage. The mechanic shook his head as he walked over to them. Thin wisps of blondish red hair danced around his balding forehead. "I told you, Lou. You need a new tire."

"Can you put one on for me?"

As Gus took the bike from Ken, Lou introduced them.

Gus shook his head at the bike. "Let me go check, Lou and see if I've got a tire to fit this. By the looks of it, you should get two new ones."

Lou sighed at the unexpected expense. But she had no choice. "Okay."

Gus propped the bike on its kickstand and disappeared into the shaded shop. Ken lingered nearby.

The mechanic returned. "I gotta send Fred across town to get you tires. Give me a couple of hours, will ya?"

Ken turned to her. "Why don't we go get something to eat? There's a diner a couple of streets away."

Lou paused a moment. With Matt gone, she hadn't felt like cooking. A meal prepared by someone else would be nice. "Okay."

He smiled, retrieved his coat and her sweater from the basket, and held out his elbow. "Shall we?"

"Where you goin'?" Gus asked. "If it ain't far, I'll bring the bicycle over to you."

"Sandy's." Ken said, then raised his eyebrows at Lou. "Will that be all right?"

Sandy's was a place for teens. Lou had eaten there once with Matt several years earlier, at Matt's request when it was still okay for him to be seen in public with his mom. Maybe the place had changed. Regardless, today she was with Ken so . . . why not?

"Sure," she answered.

It hadn't changed. Lou felt like a woman at a poker table the moment she entered the diner. She recognized several former students inside.

A few mumbled, "Hi, Mrs. Jensen," as Ken led her to an empty booth near the dance floor at the end. She would have preferred to sit at the counter but she did not want to let on how uncomfortable she felt. When Ken sat down opposite her, his wide grin indicated he was not bothered in the slightest by how much they must stand out.

"Hello, again, Ken!"

"Hi, Andy."

"Andy," Lou echoed and frowned at the young man she had taught nearly four years before.

"Mrs. Jensen! Haven't seen you in a while. Ken here has become somewhat of a regular." Lou gave the lad a stern look, which he tried to deflect by asking, "Uh, can I take your order?"

"Shall I order for us?" Ken asked.

"Sure."

Obviously familiar with the menu, Ken ordered two hamburger baskets, two orders of onion rings, and two milkshakes."

"What flavor shake would you like, Mrs. Jensen?" Andy asked.

"Uh, chocolate. And no onion rings for me."

"Vanilla for me, Andy," Ken said.

"You got it." Andy quickly walked away.

"What did the poor kid do?" Ken asked. "Forget to hand in an English paper before he went on to high school?"

"I just don't think it's proper for him to address you by your first name. After all, you're a teacher and he's still in high school."

Ken looked puzzled, then shrugged. "Guilty," he said, as he raised his right hand. "I told him to."

"As I said, you are a little strange."

She was surprised by his wide, infectious grin. "When you get to know me a little better, I'll consider that a compliment."

She laughed louder than she meant to. She looked out the window and hoped he didn't see the blush in her cheeks. She was not used to flirtation.

The jukebox blared to life with a song she had heard Matt play on his record player. But it was too loud. She resisted the urge to put her hands over her ears. Two couples got up to dance.

"Don't you love this music?" Ken asked with such happiness that Lou wondered if he was a teenager inhabiting an adult's body.

"Uh, it's okay."

"Dion."

"What?"

"Dion; that's who sings this song, "The Wanderer"." He looked extremely pleased with himself.

Definitely strange, Lou thought.

Fortunately their shakes arrived, followed by the food shortly afterward. As she was hungry, she easily finished the hamburger and fries. By that time the music didn't seem so loud. And she did enjoy watching the kids dance.

"Would you like something else?" Ken asked.

"No thank you. I'm full. I'd better do some extra bicycling tonight."

"Well . . ." A mischievous glint came into his eyes. "Your bicycle isn't here yet, so we could burn some calories on the dance floor."

"Burn some . . . what did you say, calories?"

Another puzzled look crossed his features before he hastily added, "Exercise, you know, by dancing."

"Here? You're definitely weird."

He grinned broadly and to her chagrin pulled her to her feet. "So already I've deteriorated from 'a little strange' to 'weird.' I'd better dance with you before you decide I'm dangerous."

She pulled against his hand. "No, I'll be dangerous if I try to dance." She hadn't danced since Ted died and she was painfully aware of the brace on her right hand. "Besides, in case you haven't noticed, this is a place for teenagers."

That grin again. "Who says?" He placed a hand around her waist and gently grasped her ugly, braced wrist in his other hand. The physical contact startled her and they were on the dance floor before she realized it.

He spun her about and led her into a jive to Elvis crooning, "Good Luck Charm." He halted after a few steps and said. "Would it be okay if I led?"

She laughed. Ted hadn't liked to dance and had often joked they danced better when she led. She nodded and shrugged. "It's been a long time." She ignored the stares of the students and instead focused on the unfamiliar moves.

After several repetitions she began to relax. But then Ken tried a different action. She faltered, giggled, but after a few tries got it.

The end of that song brought applause and to her surprise, Janet Leech, another former student, came up to her with a boy Lou didn't know, and asked her to show them how to do that.

"You'll have to ask Mr. O'Neil."

Ken appeared very happy to oblige. Nickels were fed into the jukebox as more couples came onto the floor to try the jive steps Ken demonstrated with Lou. By the time a waltz came on, the floor was packed. Ken pulled her close.

Her first impulse was to push away, but this was soon swallowed by an urge to get even closer.

When the dance finished, she stepped back. Only then did she realize the sun had set and it was dark outside. She looked at her watch. It was half-past eight.

"And that," Ken leaned close, "Is my clue to take you home."

She looked up at him. With any other man she would have stepped back to regain her personal space. But she felt an urge to be even closer. "I wonder if Gus was able to get my tires put on."

Ken nodded. "I saw him park your bike out front a while ago."

"And you said nothing?"

He shrugged. "He just parked it and left. I wanted to dance with you." Ken pulled a few bills from his wallet, set them onto the table, and waved at Andy.

Andy's return wave was vigorous. "Thanks Ken-er, Mr. O'Neil."

They exited to a chorus of "Thanks, Mrs. Jensen, Mr. O'Neil!"

"Mr. O'Neil," Ken mumbled as he reached for her bicycle.

"Why does that bother you? It's the proper address."

He shrugged. "It sounds so formal."

"And what's wrong with that? After all, you are a lot older than they are. Although you don't really act it," she added with a smile.

He looked at her and grinned. "Thanks! And let me remind you, you too are quite capable of dancing like a teenager."

"I must admit, I did enjoy it. Where did you learn those steps?"

The puzzled look she had seen cross his face before returned, this time laced with worry. Remembering his amnesia, she quickly apologized and reached for her bicycle. "I'd better get home."

He held onto it. "Let me walk you."

"But it's quite a distance from here."

He shrugged. "So?"

She hesitated. "Well, perhaps part of the way."

The night was clear and the air had lost its warmth with the setting of the sun. In spite of her sweater, she shivered. He leaned the bicycle against his leg, took off his coat and placed it carefully around her shoulders.

"Won't you be cold?"

He smiled and shook his head. They walked for a while, then he broke the silence by saying, "Tell me about Louise Jensen."

"What do you want to know?"

"Everything. Then I'll tell you the rest of what I know about Ken O'Neil. Which, after what I've already told you should take, oh, maybe ten seconds or so."

Lou laughed. "You're crazy."

"Aha! A new level of insanity. Good progress for a few hours I'd say."

She had meant to stop after a few blocks and ride the rest of the way home. But before she knew it, she had given him her entire history and found herself at the end of her driveway.

"How will you get back?" She asked. "I have no car."

He did a little jig. "That's what feet are for."

Thump!

The sound came from around the side of the house, beyond the fence that enclosed the back yard. By the look on his face Ken had heard it as well.

The tinkle of shattering glass was followed by a muffled oath.

Someone was breaking into her house!

TWELVE

Ken handed Lou her bicycle. "Stay here," he whispered.

Before she could get another word out, he sprinted up to the gate and peered over the fence. She set the bicycle on the grass and started to follow. Already Ken had disappeared into the backyard. As she was sure the gate creaked, he must have cleared the fence somehow.

Then, "Oof. Who the hell are you?"

Matt? Why was he home?

She raced through the gate, which announced her passage by the expected creak. Even with his scalp closely shorn, she recognized her son. Ken had him pinned to the ground, one arm twisted behind his back.

Matt yelled, "Get off me!"

"Ken, he's my son!"

Ken immediately got up. "I thought you said he was at West Point?"

Matt got to his feet and rubbed his shoulder. "Jesus, that hurt!"

"Matthew!"

Ken held his hand out. "I'm sorry, Matt, I thought you were a burglar!"

"A burglar? Who the hell are you?" He touched the bridge of his nose then looked at his fingers. "Jesus, I'm bleeding!"

"Matt! Stop swearing and come into the house so I can look at you." Lou followed her son inside with Ken at her heels.

Matt turned to look back, but Lou pushed him into the kitchen and made him sit down at the table. As she applied a tissue to his nose, her son continued to stare at Ken. "You're not very big. How'd you knock me down so easily?"

Ken shrugged. "Element of surprise."

"But where'd you come from?"

"Over the fence."

There was a bit of swelling, but Matt's nose didn't look broken and the cut was shallow. Lou gave it a final wipe. "Matt, this is Mr. O'Neil, the new history teacher."

"Oh, I'm away for two months and you got a boyfriend already? Way to go, Mom." Her son's teasing made her blush for the fourth time that night.

"Matt, what are you doing home and why didn't you use your key?"

"I couldn't find it. You didn't answer the door so I thought I'd let myself in, but I slipped and my foot went through the damn window."

"If this deterioration in your language is the only thing you learned at West Point, I'd prefer you unlearn it. Now why are you home?"

Matt sighed and studied the floor.

Ken spoke up. "I think I'd better go and let you look after your burglar, Lou."

"Nice to meet you." By Matt's grin and light tone Lou knew Ken had been forgiven.

Lou led Ken toward the door. "Thanks."

"For what – beating up your son?"

"No. Though I hope the blow knocked some sense into him – oh-oh." Through the lace curtains on the front window, she saw headlights pull to a stop in front of the house. The county insignia on the door of the car confirmed her fears.

"What?" Ken asked.

Before she could answer, footfalls thudded on the steps outside. After two quick raps, she unlocked the door. The bearlike form of her brother-in-law rushed inside.

"Have you heard from Matt?" Steve asked.

"I'm here," Matt leaned against the doorway into the kitchen.

Oh, shit, Lou thought.

Steve took three long strides and towered over her son. "I just got a call from West Point! You've been AWOL since this morning. What the hell's going on, Matt? You had me worried to death and probably your mother, too."

Matt straightened and attempted to look his uncle squarely in the eye, which was difficult, as Steve had three inches on her son. "I quit."

"You *what?*"

"I've decided to work a year, put together a portfolio, then apply for the fine arts program at Michigan State."

Steve sucked air and Lou knew he was attempting to get his infamous temper under control.

"What went wrong, Matt?" she asked as calmly as she could.

"A lot of things."

"Son," Steve began, "there's always a lot of hazing at first. You can live through it. I can call the general and see if they'll . . ."

"No!" Matt had never sounded so defiant. "I am not going back there." He looked to his mother for support. She searched for words that might diffuse the situation.

"Now look here, son," Steve began.

"I am not your son. I am eighteen years old. I can make my own decisions."

Steve's face flushed and Lou prepared herself for a verbal torrent.

"Why don't you both mull it over a couple of days?"

Ken's words surprised Lou. She had forgotten he was still there.

Steve swung about like a lion suddenly aware there was a gazelle in the cage. "And who the hell are you?"

"Mom's new boyfriend," Matt said smugly.

Steve closed the distance to Ken and leaned threateningly forward. He was nearly half a foot taller than the teacher.

Lou jumped between them. "This is —."

"No," Steve interrupted her, "let me guess. You're the new history teacher, right?"

"Ken O'Neil." Ken held out his hand. Steve didn't shake it.

Lou sighed. "This is my brother-in-law, Steve Jensen."

"Sheriff, to you," Steve said. "Now, we're in the middle of a family discussion if you don't mind . . ."

"No, we're not," Matt interjected.

Steve swung around to glare at his nephew.

"Look," Lou began. "Ken's right. Let's sleep on it and talk about it Sunday." She sent her own dart at Matt to keep him hushed. "And I'm tired. Matt must be too." She gave Steve a gentle push. "We'll see you Sunday, Steve."

Steve sighed, then to her relief, nodded. After a direct look at Matt, he turned back to Ken. "Let me give you a lift home."

"That's okay, Sheriff. It's a beautiful night."

"Oh, but I insist." Steve's blue eyes glinted and Lou knew Ken was about to be cross-examined. She resisted an urge to give her bully of a brother-in-law a kick in the shins.

"Well, in that case, I accept with gratitude," Ken responded, his voice full of mock charm. He winked at her. "I've never ridden in a police car before."

Steve stomped outside and Ken followed, but stopped at the bottom and turned to face her. "I really enjoyed tonight. Can we do it again sometime?" This time the charm was sincere.

She smiled and nodded. Before she shut the door she could hear Ken ask Steve. "Can we put the siren on?"

She hoped Steve was not at the end of his already short tether.

* * *

Steve was not in a good mood. The wiseass beside him was particularly annoying. Well, he'd soon put the jerk in his place.

"Well, that didn't take you long. You've been here what, a month?"

"Actually, two and a half months. Long for what?" Ken replied.

Brazen ass-hole. "To move in on my sister-in-law."

"Oh, we've only just started seeing each other. It'll be awhile before we move in together."

Steve took his eyes off the road long enough to glare at his passenger. The teacher met his gaze squarely and Steve was smacked with the intuition the man was not attempting to hide anything and certainly was not afraid of him.

He got straight to the point. "And just what are your intentions with Lou?"

"I'd like to get to know her a little better."

Steve took in a breath and attempted to snuff the volcano of violence threatening to erupt within him. He managed to remain silent until he pulled to a halt in front of Mrs. Lacey's house.

Then he let his suppressed rage leak into his voice as he leaned over. "You'd better not turn out to be married, mister."

"I won't."

"And I'm only going to tell you this once. You hurt Louise in any way, shape, or form and I will personally tear you limb from limb." He poured as much threat as he could into every word.

The teacher's responding look was open and unafraid. "Sheriff, as much as I am sure you would enjoy doing that very thing, you will never be given a reason to do so."

Although Steve couldn't understand it, the frank honesty of the man angered him even further. He jerked his door open. "I'm going inside with you."

"How nice. I don't often get visitors."

"Wiseass!"

O'Neil had a key to get in. Steve followed him inside. "Where's Mrs. Lacey? I want to talk to her."

"I'll go get her," came the damnably polite answer. O'Neil took the steps two at a time. Within a few minutes Mrs. Lacey came down with O'Neil grinning behind her.

"Why, Sheriff, I haven't seen you in years. How's Susan? And the girls? Getting big I bet?"

"Yes, ma'am. Susan's fine." He cleared his throat. "Could I talk to you a minute?"

"Of course."

Steve glared at O'Neil over the top of Mrs. Lacey's white hair.

"I'll go put some tea on," O'Neil said, but before heading to the kitchen he gave Steve a smile that Steve wanted to remove permanently.

"Oh, and heat up some of those muffins," Mrs. Lacey called after him. "Would you like to sit in the parlor, Sheriff?"

"Actually, I just wanted to make sure you were okay with O'Neil here. He's treating you well, is he?"

"Oh, he's an angel. He's fixed the place up so much. Come out to the kitchen. He'll have the tea made in a minute. He baked the muffins himself."

"He did?" What kind of weirdo was this guy? A thought occurred to him. "I'd better get going. O'Neil?" he called to the kitchen.

The teacher came down the hallway and feigned disappointment. "Oh, do you have to leave so soon?"

If Mrs. Lacey hadn't been present, Steve would have told the fellow where he could shove his sarcasm. "I want a word with you. Goodnight, Mrs. Lacey."

"Goodnight, Sheriff."

Out on the porch, which Steve noted had been repaired, he turned back to O'Neil. "Why don't you come to Sunday dinner with Lou and Matt?"

O'Neil looked shocked. Steve felt a flush of pleasure at catching the fellow off guard. But the man didn't hesitate long. "I'd be happy to, as long as it's okay with your wife and Lou."

"It'll be fine. You just be there. One o'clock. Eleven Pleasant Street."

"I will. Thanks for the invitation."

Steve took two steps, then turned. "Just so you know, I'm going check up on you, O'Neil."

Ken waved with enthusiasm. "That's great. Let me know what you find out."

It was Steve's turn to be dumbfounded and he felt his rage return. He spat out the word "Wiseass" and headed to his car.

As Steve sped away, his anger continued to simmer, fed by his worry about his nephew. Even if he talked Matt into returning to West Point, this would be a blemish on the lad's military record.

This was probably why he had allowed O'Neil to get under his skin. What the hell did Lou see in this guy? O'Neil was too smooth. Too glib. He definitely warranted checking out. And as the sheriff, he had resources.

O'Neil would not remain a mystery for long.

THIRTEEN

Mauston, October 19, 1962

Eighth-graders stampeded past Ken in their eagerness to leave the school for the freedom of the weekend before them. Debbie Jensen turned around and hollered, "Hi, Auntie Lou!" before she scurried after her friends. Her blond curls bobbed at the end of her ponytail. Ken turned and saw Lou leaning against her homeroom door. He closed the gap between them.

"Auntie Lou?" he questioned.

Her smile reached her eyes. She nodded.

A thought stabbed at him. "Wait – you're Debbie's aunt? That means . . ." He glanced back in the direction Debbie had fled. "I have the sheriff's daughter in my class. How lovely."

Lou giggled. "You seemed to handle him just fine the other night."

"Well, the score may be in my favor now, but that could change Sunday."

She straightened up. "Sunday? What do you mean?"

"Didn't Steve tell you? I'm invited for Sunday dinner."

"No, he did not." Her brow furrowed and he resisted a sudden urge to smooth it with his fingers.

"He probably wants to check me out – see if I qualify to date his sister-in-law. He's a tad protective of you."

Her frown persisted.

"Look, if you're uncomfortable with this, I won't go."

"Steve likes to play big brother and sometimes he goes a little too far. Once in a while he needs to be put in his place and his wife Susan is always willing to help me do just that. If you don't mind witnessing some verbal battles, I'd like you to come. And I know Matt would too."

"So your son harbors no hard feelings over our little tussle?"

"Other than a bit of hurt pride. He played football last year and being bigger than you he thought he should have been able to handle you. He wants you to show him that move of yours." She straightened up. "Well, I'd better get home. I have a ton of papers to mark. See you Sunday?"

He nodded. "Yeah, see you Sunday."

Her smile seemed to reach across the distance between them and touch him on the inside. As she walked away, he realized his attraction to her was growing stronger. Dare he let himself become involved with someone when he had no clue as to who he really was? He shook his head and returned to his classroom. He also wanted to mark some tests. Concentrate on normal activities. Try not to fall over the brink.

At least not until he had done what he needed to do, whatever that was.

* * *

October 20, 1962

Lou was the last thing on Ken's mind when he fell asleep Friday night and first in his thoughts when he woke. He looked at the clock. It was only seven-thirty. He rolled over and tried to get back to sleep, but Lou's smile lingered in his consciousness. Well, this is an improvement he thought - from obsessing about needing to do God knows what to obsessing about a woman.

He rolled over again and breathed in the fresh air coming through the small gap he had left open in the French doors.

Time for a long run, something told him. He wondered where these nagging thoughts came from. From the occasional run and the work he did around the house, he felt he kept in fairly good shape. He usually ran as far the Travel Inn on the highway and back, which, according to Andy at the diner amounted to about eight miles. He wondered how far he should go today.

The number fifteen jumped into his head like someone had planted it there. Fifteen miles? Less than a marathon, but more than half a marathon. Now why would he think that of that number? Rather than dwell on it, he got up and pulled on a pair of sweatpants and sweatshirt. Doubling his regular route would make sixteen miles.

The brisk air embraced him as he exited the house. Little seemed wrong in the quiet town under a cloudless sky and strengthening sun. He decided to keep his worries at bay and just enjoy the moment. Birds that hadn't headed south yet chirped in agreement.

The crisp temperature allowed him to maintain a good pace and he headed toward Attewell Street en route to the highway.

* * *

Lou sniffed the air. It smelled like fall. And it looked like fall, she thought as she studied the collage of colors of the trees that lined her street. She hauled her bicycle out through the gate.

It felt good to cruise on such a beautiful day. She often did this on the weekend in the early hours before the town began to stir. After Gus's latest repairs, her bicycle sailed soundlessly on the asphalt.

She looped the town, then coasted along Main Street until she came to one of the three stoplights in town. As she waited for it to turn green, she wondered whether she should return home or do another circuit. She decided she was not ready to go back yet. She took a deep breath and pedaled.

Where had this surge of energy come from? Probably her enjoyment of teaching art. But also, she conceded, some of it came from the attention she got from a certain history teacher. Just the thought of Ken created an additional pulse of energy. She decided to pedal out to the highway and back before she headed home to cook breakfast for Matt.

She had just left Grove Street and turned onto Attewell when she spotted what looked like someone running toward her. Was something wrong? Had there been an accident on the highway? She pedaled faster.

It was Ken. Running toward her. And grinning.

"Good morning," he said, then surprised her by running past her when she stopped.

"Hey!" she hollered and twisted her front wheel around.

He waved for her to follow him.

When she caught up to him, she matched his pace. He was sweating profusely and breathing hard.

"Is everything okay?"

His widened grin created multiple dimples on each cheek. "Everything just got better."

Pleasure flushed her cheeks and she rode ahead a bit so he wouldn't notice. "Why are you running?" she asked over her shoulder.

"Why are you biking?" was his answer.

"Well, it's such a beautiful day."

"Why else?" he asked.

She slowed to match his pace. "Transportation. It's how I get around. Now answer my question. Why are you running?"

"Exercise."

A black and white Ford passed them from the other direction, then slowed. Steve. Lou wasn't surprised to hear the vehicle turn around behind them. Soon it paced them.

Ken waved. "Good, morning, Sheriff!"

"Just what are you doing?"

Lou glanced at her brother-law but already knew by the tone of his voice that he was addressing Ken.

"The breaststroke."

"Wiseass! It's not even nine o'clock on a Saturday morning. What are you two doing out here?"

Ken answered first. "I'm running and Lou is biking."

"Why?" The word held little patience.

"Exercise."

"What?"

"You know, to keep in shape. Only Lou doesn't really need to."

Steve put on his flashers and pulled in front of them, forcing them both to a halt. He hauled himself out of his car and stalked toward them.

Ken held up both hands. "Now hold on, Sheriff. I had no idea there was a town ordinance against flirting with English teachers."

Lou would have giggled except for the scowl on Steve's face. "What's wrong, Steve?"

He widened his eyes at her as if she were daft. "What's wrong? I don't like the way he talks in the presence of a lady. And isn't it a little early in the morning to be seen together?"

Lou grunted in disgust, stood on her pedals, and pumped away from the scene as fast as she could, eager to escape before either man noticed the blush on her cheeks. She found Ken's compliments and Steve's response equally uncomfortable. What was it with Steve?

Just as she cornered onto Main St. Steve pulled his car up beside her.

"Are you okay?" he asked through his open window.

"Of course I'm okay," she snapped. "Why wouldn't I be?"

"Well, dammit, Lou, face it. He's a little odd. And I've called some buddies in Pittsburg. Nothing came up. The guy has no history."

"I know. He told me about his amnesia. Have you talked to Irma Wilson?"

"I did. Why in hell she would hire him under those circumstances I'll never know."

"As usual, Mrs. Wilson's instincts have served her well. Ken is an excellent teacher and his students love him."

"Tell me about it. I think Debbie has a crush on him. But you be careful, Lou. Who knows who he really is? Besides, who would go running for no reason?"

"He does it for exercise."

"He does it a lot, Lou. Lots of people have told me they've seen him out running. At all hours of the night."

"Is that a crime?" A red light brought them both to a stop.

"No, but it's dammed weird."

"Well, talk to him about it."

"He's a wiseass. I just told him I didn't like weirdos running about this town at all hours and you know what he said? 'I'll keep an eye out for you, Sheriff.'"

Lou chuckled at his poor imitation of Ken. Steve started to say something else, but his radio blared to life.

When the light turned green, Lou hollered, "See you tomorrow!" and pedaled for home.

FOURTEEN

Mauston, October 21, 1962

Jennifer's giggle trickled in through the open window. Steve paused in his dressing and looked out. Matt sat on the swing with Steve's middle daughter. She squinted up through the bright sunlight at her older cousin and hung onto his every word.

The clatter of pans from the kitchen told him his wife Susan was preparing Sunday dinner. Turkey, by the smell filtering upstairs. Lou and Matt must have come from church with Susan and the girls. Susan had let Steve play hooky from church and sleep in. Between the extra sleep and refreshing bath, he felt good. Relaxed.

Until he remembered whom he had invited for dinner.

He hurriedly buttoned up his shirt. He wanted to chat with Matt and get the West Point matter straightened out before O'Neil showed up.

When he reached the bottom of the stairs Susan greeted him with a cup of strong coffee.

She kissed his cheek. "Mmm, you smell nice and clean."

He wrapped his free arm about her waist and pulled her close. Her auburn curls tickled his chin. "Maybe you should come back upstairs with me and make sure I cleaned behind my ears."

She giggled and slapped at his hand. "Now behave yourself. I have to get dinner ready." Her eyes sparkled at the anticipation of company. He knew she liked having visitors though he could never fathom why, considering all the fuss she went to.

Her perky features sobered. "Lou's in the kitchen. Matt's waiting for you on the deck."

"Don't I get something to eat, first?" Steve sipped his coffee and, with his arm still about her waist, steered Susan into the kitchen. "Hello, what have we here?" A pyramid of freshly baked rolls sat on top of the counter. "You make these, Lou?" He dodged Susan's slaps and grabbed one. His teeth cut easily through the tender dough. "This morning?" he said with a full mouth.

Lou winked at him.

Susan swatted his shoulder playfully. "Don't talk with your mouth full and don't you dare let the girls catch you with one of those before dinner."

He swallowed. "Now don't tell me you got up early to make these for Wiseass."

This Lou ignored.

"Mom, Daddy swore on a Sunday and he's eatin' a roll!" a voice squealed from the back door. Elizabeth shook her chubby four-year-old finger at her father. She had been a surprise addition to the family and was five years younger than Jennifer, and bossier than all the other females in the house. Where her siblings were blondes, Elizabeth had bright orange hair that promised to mature into the rich color of her mother's.

Steve made a face at Elizabeth and escaped out to the back veranda. On a normal Sunday, he would relax on the sun-dressed porch with his coffee and the Saturday edition of *The Mauston Times*. But this was not a normal Sunday he decided, as he spotted Matt's tense shoulders where he hunched down in a wicker chair. Steve gobbled the rest of the roll and pulled his rocker over next to Matt.

"Mighty fine rolls your mom makes."

Matt nodded. "She was up early mixin' the dough."

"She go out on her bicycle this morning?"

Matt looked puzzled. "I don't know. Why?"

Steve sipped his coffee and shrugged. "Just wondering. You come to a decision?"

"Yes, sir."

The lad's tone hung heavy with tension. Steve took another drink of coffee and tried to ignore the impatience brewing in his gut.

Matt must have sensed his uncle's mood, as he quickly said, "Just hear me out. Please."

Steve feared his temper would grab the reins and run if he looked at Matt. So instead he focused on the lawn. Leaves had begun to litter the grass. Breathe. Relax. Stay in control. "I'm listening," he said at length.

"I'm going to pay you back the tuition money."

What control Steve had grew wings and flew away. He swung his head about and fixed the lad with a glare. "Matt, to hell with the goddamn money! It's your education I'm concerned about! How could you possibly give up an opportunity like West Point?"

"Don't you throw my good china!" Susan hollered through the kitchen window.

Matt returned Steve's glare. "It was more a prison than an opportunity."

Steve inhaled, paused, then exhaled. He forced his voice down to a reasonable level. "Look. When your daddy and I went there, we found it tough at first. All new cadets do. But when we came out of there, we were men."

Matt stood up. "I'm already a man."

Steve set his cup down a little harder than Susan would have liked and rose to his feet. "Well then you'd better start acting like it. A man wouldn't run home to his momma because of a little hazing."

"Hell, Steve. The hazing was the only fun part of the whole thing. I just don't want to become an officer." Matt spat the last sentence out as if the words tasted bad.

Steve blinked at this stranger in front of him. Matt had never called him anything but Uncle Steve and had never before spoken to him in that tone. He continued on the offensive. "How the hell can you determine that after two months?"

"Because I know!" Matt slammed a fist into his chest. "In here."

Steve inhaled forcibly and shuffled about on the veranda. He had never struck his nephew or his children, but at the moment, he sure as hell felt like hitting something. He stepped close to Matt and was impressed by how his nephew stood his ground when he must have known his uncle was about to blow his lid.

"Okay, then tell me what the hell you plan to do next year? You gonna loaf around? Hang out at Sandy's?" He let his wrist go limp and flitted his hand in the air. "Dabble in some paint?"

Matt shoved him. Hard. Steve tumbled down the steps and landed on his ass on the lawn. He sat there, shocked into immobility.

Matt hurried down after him and extended a hand. "I'm sorry, Uncle Steve. Are you all right?"

Steve just looked at him a moment. No man, including Matt's father, had *ever* pushed him. He had always been too damn big for anyone to dare try.

"Please, Uncle Steve, I'm sorry. I just lost it."

Matt looked so genuinely distressed, Steve took the lad's hand and let him help him up.

"Just don't ever talk about painting that way," Matt said. "It insults me and, worst of all, it insults my mom."

The shock had evaporated Steve's temper. "I never intended to insult you, son. And I sure as hell wouldn't dare insult your mother."

"You've got to understand, Uncle Steve. I am different from you and my father. This summer, I started to realize what I want to do, and those two months at West Point just made me more certain. I've got a job over in New Lesbon at that new grocery store. I'm going to be working whatever hours they can throw at me. I've got a friend I can stay with during the week, then I'll come home on weekends."

"Matt, how far can you go in a grocery store?"

"Hold on a moment. My paycheck will go to pay off the money you gave me for my West Point tuition. Sandra showed one of her professors some of my work. He told her that if I prepared a portfolio by next spring, I had a chance at a scholarship. When I'm not working, I plan to spend every minute with my artwork. And I happen to live with one helluva a teacher. *This* is what I want to do Uncle Steve. It is what I am *going* to do. I'm sorry, but I am not my father." He repeated the last sentence slowly.

Steve eyed his nephew and wondered how the hell the boy had grown up without him knowing it. He had to admit that Matt was right: he was not Ted. And Steve had no right to expect him to be.

He draped an arm over the lad's shoulders. "Hell, no. But you're developing a bit of a temper like your ol' uncle!" He punched Matt playfully in the gut then became serious once more. "What if your plans don't work out? What if you don't get a scholarship?"

"I'll work until I have enough money. And when I'm not working, I'll be painting."

Together, they walked back onto the porch. "What does your mother say to all of this?"

"She said to keep my options open. To keep West Point in mind if I decide I don't want to study art."

Steve clapped his nephew on the back. "A smart woman, your mother."

Debbie shouted from inside the house. "Mr. O'Neil is here!"

Steve sighed. "Now if I could just figure out what my daughter and your mother see in Wiseass."

Matt laughed. "He's all right."

Steve held the screen door open to let Matt pass. "I'm glad one of us thinks so."

* * *

Ken walked up the steps and wondered if he had been too hasty accepting the invitation. He peered through the lace curtain and saw movement. Well, he couldn't back out now. And he realized he didn't really want to. He wanted to see Lou again. And hopefully be accepted by most of her family. He didn't hold out much hope for Steve.

Debbie Jensen opened the door and gave him a shy smile. "Hello, Mr. O'Neil."

"How are you, Debbie?"

"Fine, thank you."

Lou stepped out into the hallway. The apron over her silk blouse and skirt accentuated her slim figure. "Hello," she said.

A warmth spread through him when she smiled. Yes, he definitely wanted to get to know this woman. A shorter lady stepped up beside Lou. She too had an apron on.

"Susan Jensen, this is Ken O'Neil."

Susan's handshake was firm for such a petite woman and her blue eyes looked eons warmer than her husband's.

"Hi, Ken!" Matt said.

"Hi, Ken!" echoed Elizabeth. "I'm Elizabeth!"

Ken waved. "Why hello, Elizabeth."

Debbie poked her sister in the shoulder. "Call him Mr. O'Neil."

Elizabeth's bottom lip protruded. "Matt called him Ken."

"Ken's fine," Ken said and winked at the girl who promptly winked back at him.

Steve cleared his throat. "Elizabeth, why don't you take Mr. O'Neil into the dining room?"

The young child boldly grabbed one of Ken's hands and pulled him into a room on the left.

Ken sat down and Elizabeth plunked into a chair beside him. "Debbie says you're her favorite teacher."

Ken heard a groan from the kitchen. Susan entered and led a parade of people carrying platters into the dining room. Debbie came last with the gravy, her cheeks crimson.

"Can I help?" Ken asked.

"No," Steve answered. He set the turkey down and picked up carving utensils.

Ken wasn't about to insist with the sheriff so armed.

Lou grinned and Susan frowned as they headed back to the kitchen. Matt sat down across from Ken and gave him a broad grin. The lad appeared to be intact. Obviously things had gone well during his chat with Steve.

Lou sat on Ken's right, to his disappointment. Whenever he turned to look at her, Steve was in the background, his steely eyes watching Ken's every move.

Throughout the meal, Steve said little. Elizabeth said a lot. Ken relaxed and allowed himself to enjoy the first full-course, home-cooked meal in . . . years? He did not know. It was easy to compliment the chef, who appeared to appreciate his comments.

"Lou made the rolls," Susan added.

"Well, they're not very good," Ken said as he reached for another one.

Elizabeth giggled and echoed. "They're not very good!" She also tried to reach for one. Ken picked up the plate and held it closer for her, then took another one himself. He glanced at Lou, caught her grin, then his peripheral vision caught Steve's scowl. He must like them too, Ken thought.

At the end of the meal, the girls, including Elizabeth, got up to clear the table.

Ken stood and picked up his plate.

"Leave it," Steve ordered. "The girls can manage while we adults have coffee on the veranda."

"I'll pass on the coffee and give the girls a hand," Matt said and all three of them awarded their hero with a smile.

Ken was left to uncomfortably follow the big fellow out onto the back porch while Susan and Lou poured the coffee.

"So, how's it going at school?" Steve asked.

Ken looked at Steve but the big man was studying his yard.

"It's going great."

"Yeah, Debbie says you're one of her better teachers." Steve's voice sounded cold, suspicious.

"She's one of the more attentive students."

Lou came out with a steaming cup in one hand and a cold bottle of Coca-cola in the other. She handed him the bottle. "I figured you'd want one of these."

"I do, thanks!"

Steve took a cup from Susan and sat back in his rocker. "You don't drink coffee?" His tone suggested that fact confirmed his suspicions. He pulled out a package of cigarettes and passed one to Lou. He offered one to Ken.

"No thanks."

"Don't tell me, you don't smoke? You don't drink coffee. What planet do you come from?"

"A healthy one," Susan said. "That smoke going into your lungs can't be good for you."

Steve lit Lou's cigarette, then his own, dragged deep, and blew a cloud off the veranda before replying, "Well, don't tell me that soda is better for you than coffee. I hear that stuff can take rust off a nail."

Ken said nothing and looked at Lou. She laughed and blew smoke through lips he wanted to kiss.

"What?" Lou asked. "You look like you caught me smoking in the bathroom at school."

He recovered by saying, "I didn't know you smoked."

"Nothing wrong with a lady smoking," Steve said. "Most movie stars do."

"Well don't expect me to light up because you've seen some sexy siren on the television do it," Susan teased.

Steve winked at his wife and his features softened into those of a different person. "You don't need to smoke."

Lou jumped on this. "Oh, and I do?"

"You don't need to do anything either," Ken said softly.

It was hard to tell in the deep afternoon shade, but Ken thought Lou's cheeks darkened slightly. When he saw Steve's scowl, Ken's tongue ran ahead of his brain.

"Oops, I just broke another town ordinance," for which he was rewarded with a deep throaty laugh from Lou.

Steve cleared his throat. "That reminds me, did you go running this morning?"

"As a matter of fact I did, and I still didn't see any weirdos." Ken could see Lou hiding a grin behind her cup.

"This fellow runs," Steve said to Susan. "What was it you said, Ken – for exercise?"

Ken nodded. "Chasing youth, I suppose."

"Why not join a gym?" Steve asked.

Now that sounded like a good idea. "Do they have one in town?"

"Yeah, Joe's. In the south end. I go there myself once in a while."

"What machines do they have?" Ken asked.

The looks on their faces told Ken he had said something inappropriate.

"Did you say machines?" Louise asked. In a gym?"

Ken groped for a response. "You know, equipment?"

"Oh." Steve eyed Ken closely. "The usual. Punching bag. Some weights. Ropes. And the ring, of course."

"Ring?"

"Boxing ring." Steve spoke slowly and loudly as if Ken were deaf as well as dumb.

"Boxing?" Ah, that sounded familiar.

"Yeah. You ever box?"

Ken paused. Had he? "I'm not sure."

"Well, why not give it a shot? It's good exercise."

"Okay," Ken answered.

Lou and Susan chorused with a definite "No!"

Steve ignored this and said, "How about tomorrow afternoon? I can give you an hour after work."

What the hell, Ken thought. "Sounds good. What time?"

"How about 4:30? I'll give Joe a call and book the ring."

"Do you really think it's a good idea, Steve?" Susan asked. "No one will get hurt, will they?"

"No," Ken and Steve spoke in unison and Ken thought it would be one of the few times he and Steve would ever agree. He decided that was a good time to leave.

Lou walked him to the door and from the kitchen the girls and Matt hollered good-bye all at once.

On the way home, as he strolled through the cooling late afternoon air, he could not stop thinking about Lou.

But one thought continued to pop up.

There was something he should be doing.

And going to the gym with the sheriff was not it.

* * *

Lou snuggled down beneath her quilt and listened to the drum of rain on the roof. Her thoughts drifted to the day's events and she smiled. The afternoon had gone surprisingly well. She had feared the worst: Steve hollering. Matt storming off. But Steve had accepted Matt's plans and even seemed to be in good spirits by the time Ken arrived.

She smiled in the dark. Wiseass. A cute wiseass, she thought. And Ken's quick wit had managed to stay ahead of Steve's barbs. There was one cause for worry though. Their scheduled bout the next day.

"Just what are you trying to prove, Steve?" Lou had asked after Ken left.

"What are you talking about?" Steve looked so innocent Lou wanted to smack him. "A little innovative detective work, so to speak. What better way to get to know him than to go a few rounds with him?"

"And why are you so interested in getting to know him?"

"Like I said, my buddies in Pittsburg couldn't find a thing on him. I'm only looking after your interests, Lou. I don't want you dating a murderer or some crazy lunatic. And I don't need too much more evidence to establish a case for lunacy, here."

Fortunately Steve was still sitting down and this enabled Lou to lean over him. "I can look after my own interests just fine. Why don't you butt out for once?" She looked at Susan for support.

Susan handed her another cup of coffee and smiled. "Sit down, Lou. I think Steve is concerned because of the way you look at Ken."

Lou's jaw dropped and Steve chuckled.

"And," Susan went on before Lou had a chance to formulate a response, "Steve is behaving like such a jerk because he feels no one can ever measure up to Ted and he's worried that Ken may be just the person who'll capture your heart."

Lou shut her mouth as Steve's opened.

"Face it, Steve," Susan told her husband. "It's high time Lou found someone else. And if, after tomorrow night, you don't get any bad feelings about this fellow, I want you to give him and Lou some space."

As Lou snuggled deeper beneath the blankets, she smiled at the memory of the childish pout on Steve's face. Susan had been right on both counts. Steve's memory of his younger brother had turned him into a saint and Lou did feel differently about Ken than she had any other man since her husband died. She had never imagined she'd fall in love again.

But now?

She really liked Ken. But of course, all women liked a man of mystery. No, she contradicted herself. She liked the way he looked at her. Liked the way he made her feel. Hell, she felt urges she thought had long left her body.

She went to sleep to the steady beat of rain on the roof and hoped that soon, Ken O'Neil would ask her to dance again.

FIFTEEN

Bejing, May 30, 2049

The time had come. Finally.

As Ko stepped out of the elevator, his peripheral vision caught someone standing to his left. Shimira.

She had not come to him in the five weeks of the delay. He suspected she had been sent off on a mission. With no visible emotion she saluted him. This puzzled him, as she was superior in rank to him. He returned the salute.

As she stepped past him into the elevator, he noticed two brass studs on the collar of her uniform. There should have been three. Before the doors closed her eyes softened slightly with sadness. Or was it good-bye?

He hoped he would get the opportunity to find out when he returned. Just how much he wanted that disturbed him.

He stepped through the security door and gazed upon the time chambers for the first time. They were much smaller than he had imagined. The underground lab was just a square room and the two egg-shaped chambers barely fit in it. Close together in space, but separated by eighty-seven years in time.

He bowed to his superiors, then ducked his head as he stepped inside the first chamber. The titanium door hissed like an airlock as it closed behind him.

As no metal was allowed on his person within the chamber, he would cross over the continuum with no weapons other than his own hands. But they were more than capable of completing the job in an efficient manner. O'Neil would not suffer much pain.

The scientists had worked and reworked the stolen algorithms and were certain Ko would arrive a few days before the critical event.

Ko inhaled the oxygen-rich air as deeply into his lungs as possible, then nodded at the remote camera to indicate he was ready.

Whiteness enfolded him.

Colors appeared and revolved. They became more vivid and the revolutions created a wave of nausea. Ko shut his eyes but the sensation worsened. He collapsed and vomited. His hands gripped something coarse. He opened his eyes. He was on grass. Dry brown grass.

As the spinning slowed, he heard a groan behind him. He vaulted to his feet and whirled about as his muscles coiled for attack.

The person before him resembled a withered tree branch in rags. White knuckles bulged through sun-dried skin as the man gripped the handle of a rake. As his mouth stretched into a forced tunnel, his pupils constricted. No sound made it past the pale lips before he crumpled to the ground.

Ko's brain flashed instructions to flee. He had to be at least thirty meters away. He sprinted the distance then turned to watch. The man lay on his back and stared up at the sky with the frozen expression of the newly dead.

White light obliterated the world. Color returned, but the spinning did not. The man was gone. But Ko knew the farmer had died before the transfer and this meant Ko could not return to 2049. He would never see Shimira again.

He tore that thought from his mind and focused on what he had to do. In front of him sat a small house. Its shingles had long lost their color to the sun and were cracked and split. The small porch sagged in the middle. Ko ran inside. Within seconds he found what he was looking for: a transistor radio. He turned it on. Only one station came in clearly.

Too impatient to stand there and wait, he took the radio with him and explored the rest of the house.

The architecture and décor appeared to come a time even earlier than 1962. All the interior walls were covered with patterned paper. One corner of the flowered print had started to peel. When Ko pulled on it, another pattern was revealed beneath it. And another beneath that. He could only guess how many layers had been pasted to the original sheet of gyprock.

All of the house appeared to have been constructed from flammable material. One black arm of the stove stretched through the ceiling to the upper floor while another curved into the living room. Considering the house was heated by an appliance that consumed wood, he wondered why the building had not burned to the ground long before.

The only bathroom in the house consisted of a noisy toilet and cracked sink in a closet on the back porch, as if this feature had been an add-on. There was no shower or tub. No machines in which to wash or dry clothes.

Finally the newsman announced it was four-forty-five p.m., Monday, October 22. Ko had three full days to find O'Neil. Find him and kill him.

Then, in order to prevent further contamination of the time line, Ko would also have to cease to exist.

But he welcomed death, as he would never see Shimira again. Even if he had been able to return to 2049, she would not been part of his life. Intelligence must have learned of their affair. In the last five weeks, she had not come to him, except that last day, at the elevators. The two buttons on her collar told him she had accepted demotion, and had chosen her career over him. Goodbye, that is what he had read in her eyes. Perhaps sadness too. But definitely goodbye.

So he would die here, in 1962. But at least he would have the honor of sacrificing himself to protect the future of his beloved China.

And in doing so, he would also protect Shimira's future, whatever that may be.

* * *

Mauston, October 22, 1962

Ken looked at the street sign. Pine Street. He walked slowly, not because he feared he would walk by the building, but because he feared he would find it. Sure enough. Two blocks down, sticking out from the brick wall like a lawyer's shingle, hung a sign that read: Joe's Gym. Beneath the words was a caricature of a set of boxing gloves. They reminded Ken of a skull and crossbones.

Why he felt uneasy, he wasn't sure. Something just didn't feel right. He looked up at the sign. Boxing. What could be wrong with that? Something tugged at the fringe of his memory, but not hard enough to establish a link.

He walked in. It was a lot darker than he had expected and the air was heavy with the smell of stale sweat. The gym consisted of one large room with the ring dominating the center. A punching bag hung next to a ball currently hammered by a hunched-over, thin young man. Skipping ropes adorned one wall. In the opposite corner a press bench and a few dumbbells finished off the décor.

"Well, hi ya, sport!" Steve came over and slapped Ken roughly on the shoulder.

Wiseass to you, Ken thought, but kept his lips sealed, which he had decided was the best way to get on this fellow's good side.

"Locker room's this way."

Steve led Ken down a dingy hallway into an equally dingy room. It had one bench, half a dozen lockers, and a doorway to what looked like a shower stall. Ken was glad he had brought clothing like Steve's: T-shirt, shorts, and sneakers. However, as they retraced their steps back to the main area, the feeling that all was not right grew stronger.

"Want to warm up, first?" Steve asked.

"Sure," Ken said, for lack of a better answer. He pulled down a rope, adjusted the length, then found an open area. Would he know how to do this? Or was he about to become the cheapest entertainment in town? He turned his back to the room and gave it his best shot.

To his relief, skipping came to him as naturally as dancing. He increased the speed to get his heart rate up, then alternated between slow and fast, worked with the one-two step, and then wrapped it up with some crossovers. Sweating and loosened, he turned to see everyone watching him.

"Not bad," Steve said in a tone that said, so what? He threw two gloves at Ken. "Here, put these on. Mel will help you lace up."

Mel was an older man whose eyes checked Ken out while he automatically laced up the wrists of the gloves. "Hopefully you can box as good as you can skip," he said. "The sheriff doesn't do too bad for an out-of-shape amateur."

Thanks for the warning, Ken thought as he climbed into the ring. The lighting there was the most efficient in the place. Once inside the ropes Ken felt his mood lift a little. Yeah, this felt familiar.

Steve ducked between the ropes. He moved nimbly for a big fellow. "You ready, sport?"

Ken nodded.

"You want me to time you three minutes, Sheriff?" Mel asked from the side.

"Nah, let's just play awhile." Steve covered his lower face with his gloves; his steely eyes glinted above them.

Ken moved forward. Steve threw a straight right, which was easy enough to deflect. Steve had a good six-inch reach over him and Ken found himself on the defensive most of the time. But he had no trouble blocking the few combinations Steve tossed at him.

"Come on!" Steve growled. "Hit me!"

Ken shot a jab to the big man's jaw, but it did not land. The sheriff rallied with a combination right, left, and right hook, but none of these found the mark either.

To Ken's relief, Steve's breathing grew labored. This however, did not cause the sheriff to lessen the strength of his blows.

Steve's temper flared in his voice. "Come on, is that all you got? Let's box, not flit around like a couple of women!"

Steve increased his assault and Ken continued to thwart the attack, but the big man advanced as he swung and Ken was forced to step back.

Ken found himself against the ropes. He ducked a roundhouse and stepped sideways into the center of the ring. He was tiring a bit himself, and with each blow the bull-headed sheriff came closer to landing one. If he did, Ken knew he would be consuming only milk shakes at Sandy's for the next month.

"Dammit!" Steve hollered. "C'mon you pansy-ass dancer. Show me what you got." He swung.

Ken curled to the left as Steve's glove grazed his right ear. He saw an opening and swung in a 360-degree arc, pushed off with his right foot, and became air-borne. In mid-flight he brought his left leg hard across his body and his foot made contact with Steve's left temple.

The big man crumpled like a deck of cards.

Yes! Ken tried to contain his exuberance.

Steve looked up at him, disbelief written all over his face.

Of course. Steve hadn't expected that, had he?

Mel climbed into the ring and applied a towel to the blood running down Steve's cheek. The old man looked up at Ken in disgust.

"You kicked him!"

Steve glared up at Ken and his shock twisted into anger. "You kicked me! I don't believe it! You kicked me."

Uh-oh, Ken thought. What had felt so right, so perfect, a moment ago now seemed so *wrong*. He knelt beside Steve.

"Are you all right?"

"No!" bellowed Steve.

"You're going to need stitches, Sheriff." Mel said. "I'll drive you over to Doc Avery's."

Mel held the towel to Steve's head as they climbed out of the ring.

"Can – can I do anything to help?" Ken asked.

"No! Just stay away from me. Jesus Christ! I can't believe he kicked me!" Steve's last words faded as the door closed behind the two men.

Ken avoided the stares of the others as he went into the locker room. He sat down and saw blood on the heel of his left sneaker. He should have been barefoot, he thought, then immediately wondered where that idea had come from. He gave his head a vigorous shake but that failed to clear the muddle.

So much for letting the sheriff get to know him a little better. If they became any better friends, Ken would most likely end up behind bars. Or in a padded room in a straightjacket.

Ken quickly changed and exited without looking at anyone. The wind had turned cold and he pulled the lapel of his sport coat up to keep some of the chill off his neck.

He turned up Main Street. Ahead of him a crowd looking through the windows of Weir's Appliances blocked the sidewalk. Two televisions were on.

Ken managed to squeeze close enough to peer over the head of a short lady. Puzzlement over the black and white screen evaporated when he saw who was speaking. Cold fear coursed through him as John F. Kennedy addressed the nation. Any thrill of actually seeing this great man on live television was extinguished by the president's announcement of the discovery of the installation of Soviet missile sites in Cuba. Sickened, Ken maneuvered clear of the crowd.

There was something he had to do. What? It was close, oh so close. But as the nausea brewing in his stomach increased, only one thing remained clear.

Nuclear war was imminent.

SIXTEEN

On a farm outside Mauston, October 23, 1962

Ko turned onto his side in an effort to find a comfortable spot on the lumpy sofa. A damp chill spread through him, but he was reluctant to risk burning the house down by using the woodstove. Since he arrived in 1962 he had experienced something that had never plagued him before: fatigue.

As he lay there an image of Shimira came to him. He did not allow it to linger. He lurched to his feet and went into the kitchen. He put a pot of water on the electric stove and while waiting for it to boil, found the sharpest knife in the drawer. It was small, not dinnerware, but something probably used to pare vegetables.

He boiled it several minutes. Then he returned to the sofa, removed his jeans, and allowed himself six short cuts on the inside of his thigh. Each one slowly drawn to allow the tingle of pleasure to linger.

Although still tired, he knew he would not be able to sleep further. After blotting the wounds with a tissue, he began a routine of calisthenics followed by yoga. By then it was mid-morning, and another hunger arose; he needed sustenance.

What carbohydrates the farmer possessed were the worst kind: simple sugars and starches. Thankfully, there was some stock of protein: beans, which he consumed three cans of the night before. But no vegetables or fruit. No wonder the man had died of a heart attack. Or so he guessed.

He lifted the filthy curtain above the sink with his elbow and peered out at the overcast skies. He'd better get into town before the rain came. Getting wet wouldn't bother him, but he might appear conspicuous if he strolled in the rain without proper attire.

His stomach rumbled. While in town, he could shop for some nutritious food while he kept an eye out for O'Neil.

Although Ko knew how to operate a vehicle, he would not use the farmer's truck as someone might recognize it. Besides, he would enjoy the run.

When he first entered the outskirts of town, it appeared to be deserted until he reached the grocery store. Through the glass windows, he could see the lineups at the three tills extended down into the aisles. Unless he wanted to spend several hours in line, he wouldn't be buying anything.

He walked out and was surprised to find a lot of the other shops closed. As he passed a young fellow who stood on the corner selling papers, he halted. The name "Kennedy" caught his eye. From a distance he scanned the front page. Of course. The Cuban Missile Crisis.

Ko wondered if he should just wait to ambush O'Neil at the airfield on Thursday. But that would mean waiting two more days, and the last thing Ko felt like doing was sitting idle.

He noticed a sign on a lamppost that pointed to the Mauston Bus Depot. Perhaps someone there had seen O'Neil. It was worth investigating.

Once at the depot, he approached the young woman behind the wicket and described O'Neil.

She shrugged and chewed her gum harder, as if that would improve her memory. "A lot of people coming through here look like that." She blew a bubble then burst it with a loud *snap!* "You could talk to Sheriff Jensen. He keeps on top of things. His office is next to City Hall on Main Street."

Ko left the annoying female and walked outside. He had no intention of consulting the local law enforcement. This was a small town. Surely it would not take long to find O'Neil. As he strolled through town, a steady rain began that soon soaked through his clothes.

Reluctantly, he decided he would head back to the farm and satiate his hunger with more beans. If he started thinking about Shirmira, he could always return to the knife.

* * *

In the staff room, Lou poured herself a cup of coffee. Judging by its aroma and texture Jim Cage had brewed it. She hoped its potency would lift her mood a little. She'd just gotten off the phone with Matt. He had refused to come home – the store had asked every employee to work extra hours. He tried to reassure her that everyone was over-reacting and that he would be home on Saturday.

Although every teacher at the school had showed up for the eight o'clock bell, so many students were absent that at noon Principal Wilson dismissed those attending and called this emergency staff meeting.

Ken sat down across from Lou and attempted a weak smile. The despondency on his face matched how she herself was feeling.

Jim sauntered into the room. "Good afternoon!" His cheerful tone and animated movements meant he had already sampled some of the coffee he'd brewed. He refilled his cup then parked his broad frame directly in front of Ken. "Well, hello. Quite a match you and the sheriff put on, from what I hear."

Ken blinked up at Jim. "That depends on who you talk to."

"But there's something I don't get." Jim scratched his head. "Now the sheriff is about my height, if not a little taller. From what I hear you kicked him above the eye."

The banter in the room died into an expectant silence.

Ken's eyes turned as cold as his tone. "Your point?" This was not the charming man Lou was used to.

"Bear with me on this." Jim appeared oblivious to this change in Ken. "I'm really curious. Stand up, would you? Please."

Ken stood up. He was at least five inches shorter than Jim.

Jim set down his cup and grabbed a paper cone from the water cooler. "Now, for you to kick Steve in the forehead you would have to . . . let's see." He placed the paper cone at the level of his hairline. "You would have to be able to kick all the way up here." He frowned. "Is that possible?"

Ken smiled coldly and a glint came into his eyes. "I'll show you." He took the cone from Jim and placed it in the center of the big man's head. "Now, whatever you do, don't move."

Jim's eyes widened. "Wh-what—?"

"Shh!" Ken interrupted him. "I have to concentrate." Ken stepped back a few feet. He was into his second stride when Principal Wilson came through the door. Ken spun about and sat down in his chair as smoothly as if that had been his intention all along. The audience, including Lou, let out a collective breath. She noticed more than a few disappointed faces, except Jim who still stood wide-eyed like a deer caught in headlights. Lou wondered if Ken would really have tried to kick the paper cone off.

Jim retrieved his coffee cup and sat down with the cone still perched on top of his head.

Mrs. Wilson was as observant as usual. "Mr. Cage, however appropriate it may be, would you please remove your hat?"

Jim's eyeballs rolled upward, and then with a sheepish grin swiped the cone away.

Mrs. Wilson waited until the giggles died down before she continued. "I'm afraid we have more serious matters to discuss. I just got off the phone with Sheriff Jensen. In the wake of last night's presidential telecast, a lot of the townspeople have elected not to go to work in favor of stocking up on groceries and the like. Mrs. Moore has fielded numerous calls from parents inquiring if school will continue as scheduled.

"They have been informed that, as of tomorrow, students are expected to attend. Tomorrow morning at nine o'clock we will hold the assembly we'd planned for next week. We'll show a film describing procedures to follow in the event of a nuclear attack. I recommend that those of you who have not yet viewed the film be present at the assembly."

"Is that the film where the kids duck under the desks and cover their heads?" Jim asked.

"That is correct," Mrs. Wilson answered.

"As if that would make a difference," Ken said.

"Pardon me, Mr. O'Neil?"

Ken stood up. "Do you think that getting a child to duck under his desk will actually protect him from a nuclear blast?" His dark eyes challenged everyone in the room, including Mrs. Wilson.

"If a child covers his head, maybe he won't be blinded. But the resulting fireball will incinerate everything. From even three miles away, the child's clothing will ignite. His exposed skin will carbonize. And even if this child were far enough away to escape the fireball, he would be pulverized by the shock wave moving at seven hundred miles per hour, destroying everything in its path. If concrete and steel crumble, think what would happen to delicate human tissue? Then, if by some miracle, the child is far enough away to survive all of the above . . ." Ken paused and looked at each of them in turn.

Lou caught her breath when his cold gaze swept over hers.

He went on. "How could this child survive the radioactive fallout and the nuclear winter created by the massive clouds? A winter in which all plant life would be destroyed?"

Even Mrs. Wilson was shocked into silence.

Jim found his voice first. "But at least he won't end up speaking Russian. I think the government is doing the right thing. If fact, I don't think they should wait. I think they should blast the bas—" He glanced hastily at Mrs. Wilson. "Blast the Russians right now. Why wait for them to strike first?"

Ken stared at Jim. When he spoke his voice had lowered, but his crisp diction made his words come out like bullets. "Don't you realize what you are saying? Since the end of World War II both countries have made sure that if they get nuked, the enemy doesn't survive either."

Lou realized she still held her breath. Ken had mesmerized everyone and it even took Jim a moment to recover.

"Shoot, Kenny, we're too smart for that. But why would we expect anything else from you? You're more of a dancer than a fighter, right?" The big man looked pleased with himself, but no one laughed.

Ken sat down.

Mrs. Wilson stood up. "Perhaps if we had more dancers than fighters in Washington, Mr. Cage, our nation might not be in this crisis. Now, let's get through this meeting. Then we can all go home."

Lou found it hard to concentrate for the rest of the meeting. Ken's speech had been frighteningly convincing. And she could not shrug off the feeling that he knew something the rest of them did not.

* * *

Ken used the key Mrs. Lacey had given him and entered the house. Rhythmic tapping greeted him from above. Her finger cadence had picked up speed and developed a level of urgency. As if she couldn't get the words onto paper fast enough.

Most likely she hadn't bothered to eat lunch. He looked out the window as he opened a can of tuna. The sky had clouded over and daylight had dimmed. A perfect match for his mood. He took the sandwich and a glass of milk up the stairs.

He knocked on the door and the tapping stopped. "Come in."

When she spun around in the chair he noticed a glow to her face. She looked ten years younger.

"I'm sorry. You're in the middle of something," he said.

"Thanks to you, I've had more energy and always seem to be in the middle of something. Is it suppertime already?"

"No. It's just a little after one. School was dismissed early today – a lot of parents elected to keep their children home. I assume you didn't eat lunch, in spite of your promise to do so." He attempted to keep his tone light.

She frowned. "Kenneth, what's wrong?"

He tried to smile. "Other than half of the country being wiped out with a nuclear bomb, nothing." He started at the certainty in his own voice. Why would he say half? Why not a third or a quarter?

Mrs. Lacey looked at him, her pale eyes absorbing everything. "My, your sense of humor has taken a turn for the worst. Do you really think the president will allow a nuclear confrontation?"

He shrugged. "Things happen." What could happen? What should he be doing?

"Well, then. If you'll excuse me, Chicken Little, I'd better get as much writing done as I can before the sky falls in."

He said nothing and turned to leave.

"Kenneth O'Neil, stop right there." She pointed to the edge of her bed. "I was just joshing, you know. Sit down and talk to me while I eat my lunch like a good girl."

He wearily sat down.

"Have you eaten?" she asked.

He shrugged guiltily. "I'm not hungry."

Her pale eyes studied him. "Some memories returning are they?"

"I wish. All I know is there's something I should be doing."

"The news is filled with gloom and doom. What good citizen doesn't wish he could be doing something? But what can be done? Our fate lies in the hands of people in Washington, one of whom I voted for in 1960. In spite of his youth, I have great confidence in that young man. I can sense his goodness as surely as I sense yours."

But Ken's frustration had keened its edge. He stood up.

"I'm going for a run."

"But it's going to rain."

Her concern touched him. "I won't melt." Unless a nuclear bomb goes off, he thought.

"Well, don't catch cold and get something to eat when you get home."

"I will."

The tapping resumed before he reached the top of the stairs.

The rain started before he finished his first mile, but it felt cleansing, as if it was able to wash away some of his inner turmoil. By the time he returned home he figured he'd run nearly sixteen miles, in just over two and a half hours. An unexplained satisfaction filled him, as if he had reached some milestone he had been seeking.

But answers to so many questions still remained beyond his reach.

SEVENTEEN

October 24, 1962

Ken stood at the back of the gymnasium behind rows of children's heads. The entire audience was engrossed in the film. On the screen a man fell into a culvert and put his hands over his head.

The uselessness of it filled Ken with despair. Nauseated, he stepped out into the hallway then walked to the water fountain and sipped the tepid water. The dull taste did not ease the sick feeling in his gut.

"Are you okay?" Lou stood beside him.

He shrugged. "Not really."

"Are you remembering anything?"

He shook his head, "Not really." The concern on her features washed warmth through him. He did not want anything bad to happen to this kind, beautiful woman. An urge to kiss her overcame him. He grabbed her hand and led her into the nearby maintenance room.

He pulled on the overhead cord and a lone bulb revealed brooms, buckets, and mops piled neatly against the wall. With the door shut, the smallness of the room forced them closer. Her green eyes were wide. Fear? Excitement? He wasn't sure which.

He knew if he hesitated any longer he would lose his nerve, so he lowered his head and kissed her. Long. Slow. Deep.

He leaned back to gauge her reaction.

She looked startled.

Regret erased his euphoria from the kiss. "I'm sorry. It was something I had to do." Before it's too late, he thought. He tried to mask how much this last thought bothered him as he turned to leave.

But before he could open the door, she yanked him around and this time she kissed him. Her body pressed against his and he could feel her warmth through her clothes. Their kiss deepened. He felt himself harden and feared she would notice so he pulled back.

"I'm sorry," she said, though her eyes did not look apologetic. "That was something *I* had to do."

She wanted him. As much as he wanted her.

They could hear doors open out in the hallway and the clamor of children rose and fell.

"We'd better . . ." she began.

He nodded and turned to leave, but she tugged on his arm.

"Why don't you come over tonight? I could cook us supper."

She wanted to be with him. Just a moment before everything had seemed so hopeless. Now he felt anything was possible. He nodded, then opened the door for her. He waited a few seconds before he exited. There she was, down the hallway, a smile on her face. He could not help but smile in return.

"I'm glad to see you're feeling better, Mr. O'Neil." Principal Wilson stood right at his elbow. He wondered how long she had been there when she answered his thoughts by saying as she walked away, "Your trip to the storage room was obviously beneficial."

* * *

Ko slowed to a walk as he entered the outskirts of town, this time from the west. Surely today he would find O'Neil.

This morning, some of the stores had re-opened and there were more people about. When he reached the other side of town, he came upon a garage station. He was tempted to go in and ask about O'Neil when the smell of food teased his nostrils and tormented his empty stomach. He followed it until he came to Sandy's, an odd looking restaurant. He hesitated at the doorway.

All of the patrons were adolescents. They turned to look at him, but, to his relief, they quickly went back to their chatter and horrible music.

"Can I help you?" A middle-aged man spoke from behind the counter. His nametag read 'Sandy Wilson.' The owner, no doubt. His tone was cold, suspicious, as if he'd rather Ko left without ordering.

Ko stepped up to the counter and studied the menu posted on the wall. The choice consisted of simple carbohydrates and deep-fried protein. Maybe China didn't have to worry about these Americans after all. Judging from their diet, they should all eventually die of diabetes and elevated cholesterol.

The owner grunted in disgust at Ko's dalliance and went into the back. A young waitress stepped up to the counter. She was young and she too snapped chewing gum. Ko ordered the fish and chips, the hamburger basket, and a Coca-cola. He extinguished any guilt at what he was about to eat with the thought that in two days he would no longer have to worry about pending health issues.

His food arrived surprisingly fast. He found the taste of the food odd, its texture foreign. But he was hungry and surprised himself by eating everything. By the end, he even enjoyed it. He knew he would get a sugar high and subsequent low, but it would be his last meal. From now on he would consume only water. Purge his body of the contaminants to prepare his temple for the departure of his soul the very next night, right after the planes took off.

He paid the waitress, took his change, and headed toward the door. Just before he stepped outside, he heard one of the teens say, "That's how Mr. O'Neil and Mrs. Jensen did it."

Ko froze. Was it possible that O'Neil hadn't chosen an alias? The Americans had been in the process of destroying the time chambers when the Chinese overran the bunker. So most likely O'Neil did not expect anyone could follow him into the past.

Ko let himself smile. While this would be his last, and most important mission, this could also could prove to be his easiest.

With the smile still on his face, he approached the young couple. "Excuse me."

They paused in their dancing and stared up at him.

"I'm a friend of Mr. O'Neil. Do you know where I can find him?"

The boy shrugged.

"I know," said a young man at the counter. "He's probably still at school, but I know where he lives."

Ko walked over to him. "Would you write out the address for me?"

"Sure."

The young man also gave directions.

Ko easily located the house he was looking for. A tapping sound came from the upper floor. He stole around to the back, and using a thin piece of wood, slid the hook off the screen door. The inside door was unlocked. He stole inside and silently roamed the house. Except for an old lady pounding away on a typewriter, the house was empty. He went back outside and disappeared into the shadows of the ballpark, determined to wait until O'Neil returned home.

Just the possibility that this O'Neil could be the man he was searching for infused Ko with an energy that coiled and begged to be sprung.

EIGHTEEN

Ken knocked on Lou's door. He felt nervous and elated, anxious and impatient all at once. He had racked his brain the past two hours trying to remember what he was supposed to be doing. Well, until he figured that out, he decided to enjoy life as much as he could. And right now that meant being in the company of Louise Jensen.

She looked so happy when she opened the door he wanted to embrace her right there and then. But he managed to control himself and followed her to the kitchen.

She handed him a bottle of wine and a corkscrew. "I tried to stop at the store on the way home, but the lineups were so long, I decided to come right home."

She opened the refrigerator door. "Too bad Matt won't be home until the weekend. He has set some groceries aside for me. He thinks everyone is over-reacting to this Cuban situation."

They're not, Ken wanted to say, but didn't.

Lou sighed as she studied the fridge. "So, you have a choice, left-over meat loaf or a TV dinner."

"Meat loaf sounds good. I've never eaten a TV before."

"What?" She swung around and frowned at him.

Inappropriate, he thought. He looked for distraction in the bottle of wine in his hands. "Ah," he said. "1954. A very good year."

She stared at him a moment, then turned away. He set the wine on the table and pulled her around to face him. She smiled, but he saw sadness linger in her eyes.

Still holding her arms, he said, "Oh God, Lou. Was, was that the year Matt's father died?"

She shook her head. "No." She sighed and her gaze fell to her splint.

He cradled her right arm in his hands. He raised it slowly to his lips and kissed the back of her hand.

She gasped. "You must have found the one spot that still has sensation."

He gently turned the hand over and kissed the fingertips. "Can you feel that?"

She shook her head.

He kissed the spot in her palm that was exposed between the two straps that held the brace on. "Feel that?"

She pressed her lips together and shook her head.

He kissed the open area above the strap over her wrist. "That?"

Her eyes widened slightly. "I-I'm not sure," she said in a near whisper.

He kissed the soft flesh a few inches higher. "That?"

She nodded slightly and a smile tweaked the corners of her lips. Her eyes gleamed with a new brightness. Her breathing quickened.

He straightened her elbow and kissed the smooth hollow and gently sucked. "That?" he whispered.

A low moan escaped her. "Oh, definitely!" She pulled him to her with her free arm and kissed him on the mouth. In her kiss he sensed a burning need that fueled his own. She grabbed his hand and together they ran up the stairs.

Once in her bedroom, she hesitated again.

"It's okay," he said. "We don't have to do anything." Though he really, really wanted to.

She sighed, clearly fighting an internal battle.

He touched her cheek. "I can wait until you are ready," he said.

"No, it's just - it's just that I - I have more scars."

He smiled down at her. "I can't wait to kiss them."

She let out a breath of air and grappled at the buttons on his shirt. He fumbled with the zipper at the back of her dress and she laughed, her eyes sparkling with a desire and anticipation that fed his own.

Minutes later, they lay entwined, naked, sweating, still panting. He reached for the quilt and covered them both. He could not remember feeling so good, so right.

"Thanks," he said.

She tilted her head in puzzlement. "What did you say?"

"Thank you." He gently removed a strand of hair from her cheek. "For making me feel whole."

Tears swelled in her eyes. Concerned he had said something that hurt her, he started to speak, but she cut him off with a finger to his lips.

"It's okay. It's just . . . that - that's exactly how you made me feel. For the first time since . . ." She held up her still splinted wrist. "Thank *you*!" Two large tears rolled down her cheeks.

He kissed them away and this led to a slower, more intimate lovemaking. Afterward she sat up. "I'm hungry!"

"Oh?" He groaned. "I'm sleepy."

She teased his chest hairs with her index finger. "We could go down to the kitchen, have something to eat, then come back up here to . . . sleep." Her eyes shone again but not with tears.

He abruptly rolled over, began to dress, and said, "Come to think of it, I am hungry." And was rewarded with another soft laugh.

"What can I do to help?" he asked once they reached the kitchen. He was anxious to return upstairs.

"Meatloaf's in the fridge, on the bottom shelf. Stick it in the oven while I cut up some tomatoes and cucumbers."

He pulled out the small roaster and lifted the lid to inspect the half loaf. "Why don't we just pop it in the microwave?"

"The what?"

Her tone made him look at her. A mixture of puzzlement and worry creased her features.

"What's a-a microwave?" she asked.

He shook his head. "I don't know," he answered honestly.

She took the roaster from him and placed it in the oven. "It won't take long to heat up." She flipped the radio on and gave him a smile that said everything was all right. Soft music filled the room. "Dance with me?" she asked.

They waltzed to a woman crooning, "If you should lose me, you'll lose a good thing . . ." He held her tightly and believed every word of the song. The announcer informed them it was Barbara Lynn who had serenaded them. He leaned back and looked at Lou.

"Do you think I'm crazy?"

She smiled and nodded. "Perhaps. A little weird, at least."

The radio blasted out the next song: "If I had a hammer, I'd hammer in the morning…"

Ken grabbed Lou and swung her into a vigorous jive around the table. He sang along with the radio, pleased with the smooth sound of his own voice and the smile it brought to Lou's lips. He could sing. He knew the words. All of them. She giggled as he sung and laughed hard when the song ended.

"Oooh, a man of many talents!"

The DJ sounded happy as well. "That, folks, was the just-released single by Peter, Paul, and Mary. Yes, you heard it here first on WKFY, the station that'll bring you the latest to hit the . . ."

Lou shut the radio off and woodenly turned to Ken. Fear had frozen her features.

He felt nauseated. How had he known every word of a song just released? He could only shake his head.

"You knew the words . . . how could you possibly know all the words to that song?" She backed away from him, both hands reaching behind her for the cupboard, as if feeling for something solid.

He didn't know what bothered him more, him not knowing the answer or her fear of him. "Believe me, I don't know," he pleaded.

She turned around and looked out the window.

He couldn't blame her for being scared. "I-I guess I should leave."

She said nothing. She continued to stare outside as if she hoped the answer was out there.

He wished he could say something, anything that would explain what had happened. That would make things seem less crazy. But how could he, when he had no idea himself?

So, he left. Rain sprinkled down on him and light from the street lamps made everything glisten. But inside he felt only dark emptiness that gave birth to a raging frustration. What the hell was going on?

The rain steadied but it could not wash away the fire within him.

He began to run.

* * *

Lou didn't move for several minutes. Who the hell was this guy? Why did he say and do such strange things? And why did that scare her so? The rhythmic rain held no answers. No longer hungry, she reached over and shut the oven off. She felt tired and wanted to go to bed and escape into sleep.

She stopped and looked at her reflection in the window. This was what she had done after Ted's death. And it had been her first line of defense after the accident. Both times she had slept through her depression only to learn in the end that sleep had not solved anything. She had wasted weeks only to realize she had to face the problem before she could move on.

God, she wished she could understand Ken. He had frightened her with his premonitions about the threat of nuclear war. And then he'd excited her with his need to kiss her. He had put her on top of the world only to knock her off with his weird singing and comments.

She recalled the anguish on his face just before he left. He didn't have any answers either. She remembered Steve had said Ken looked bewildered after he had kicked Steve – as if he'd also surprised himself. Maybe Ken was a nut.

No. Lunacy did not explain that Ken knew every word to a song that had just been released. Fatigue tugged at her but she forced herself to look at the issues.

Could he be dangerous? Possibly.

Should she stay away from him? Probably.

Was she afraid of him? No. Not really.

Her green eyes looked back at her from her reflection.

How did she really feel about this man?

Defiance flashed in her eyes. She was in love with him.

And *that* was what really scared her.

She bolted to the front door and flung it open. The rain was heavy now. She grabbed a slicker. She pulled her bicycle through the gate and pushed off. She did not want to think, did not want to question whether or not this was the right thing to do.

But she would be there for him.

Surely together, they could find the answers.

NINETEEN

Breathless from his long sprint, Ken slowed to a stop. His shirt clung to his skin. He had left his jacket at Lou's. He dared not return for it until he had some answers. She deserved no less.

He crossed the street and headed into the park. As he passed through the shadow cast by a large oak, a black form leapt out at him. Some pre-learned instinct kicked in and he dodged the foot aimed at his head.

His foe was larger, taller, and definitely fit. The attacker dealt him a barrage of blows. Ken was able to deflect most of them. He did not have time to wonder how he knew to defend himself.

Within a minute, Ken felt his movements slowing with fatigue. He would have asked what the attacker wanted if he had any spare air to voice the question.

A well-timed heel cracked ribs on the left side of Ken's chest. He buckled with pain then spun away from the next blow. His opponent's miss gave him an opening and he aimed for the man's jaw.

But his attacker was swift. He dodged the blow, twisted to the right, grabbed Ken's wrist with one hand and locked Ken's upper arm beneath his. After one swift jerk Ken heard his elbow pop. Excruciating pain shot up into his neck.

Ken kicked into the man's back and fell away. His dislocated right elbow dangled loosely. With his left arm, Ken managed to block a foot aimed at his head, but the blow forced him backward. He only saw a brief blur before his head snapped sideways and the ground smacked into his face.

He got onto his knees and pushed against the ground in an effort to stop the world from spinning. Warm liquid ran down from his left temple and dripped off his chin onto the back of his hand.

He looked up. As the man strode toward him, Ken read a deadly purpose in the black eyes. Two long strides, then a quicker step. The man was about to deal his final blow.

And there was nothing Ken could do to stop him.

* * *

Pellets of rain bit into Lou's face. She slowed for the corners so she wouldn't skid on the slick surface. Ken must have run, she thought. Surely she should have caught up to him by now. She rounded the last corner and saw two figures in the park. One was on his knees. His right arm dangled at an odd angle.

Ken? Oh, God!

The other man stalked towards Ken. His posture, his movements told her he intended to kill him.

Lou stood on the pedals and sprinted as hard as she could. She screamed and the man looked up at her just before the collision. It felt like she hit a brick wall. She went over the handrails and tumbled in the wet grass. By the time she figured out which way was up, she could see the man was already on his feet. He looked at her, then at Ken.

Lou screamed again. A porch light came on across the street and she yelled, "Call the sheriff!"

When she looked back, the man had disappeared. She hurried over to the crumpled form of Ken. He was unconscious. She yelled again. "Call an ambulance!" The last word barely made it past her constricted throat.

She cradled Ken's head in her lap and tried to locate the pulse in his neck. But her hands trembled too much. "Hurry," she cried to no one in particular. "Please hurry!"

* * *

Back at the farm, Ko did something he had never done before. He screamed in frustration. At the sky. At the rain. At the world. He screamed long and hard, until his throat became raw. He had never failed before to cleanly assassinate someone.

Ko shuddered with nausea. He had not expected O'Neil to have any knowledge of martial arts or self-defense. Two or three blows should have been enough. But it had taken more than that and he knew O'Neil would be in pain until he was permanently put to rest.

Where had that woman come from? Ko had considered shoving her aside and finishing the job. But she had screamed and involved someone else and he could not risk further contamination of the timeline for China, and more specifically, for Shimira.

Ko allowed himself a calming breath. Shimira would have enjoyed the encounter. She would have enjoyed it even more if she had been the afflicter. With effort, he shoved her from his mind with a promise to allow himself to dwell on her later, after he completed his mission.

He would get the best opportunity to kill O'Neil when the American went to the airfield the next night. Because of his injuries, O'Neil would not be able to cover the distance on foot and would need to take a vehicle. As there was only one road to the airfield, it would easy enough for Ko to set up an ambush with the farmer's truck.

This time there would be no mistake.

* * *

The ambulance lurched as it cornered a tight bend on its way to the hospital. The wail of the siren throbbed in Lou's ears. Ken lay still upon the stretcher.

The attendants began to cut his left sleeve so they could start an intravenous. Ken began to mumble and shift about. He struggled to sit up. He tore off the oxygen mask and screamed, "Liisssa!"

The agony of the elongated name ripped through Lou's heart. Who was Lisa and what did she mean to Ken? A lot, she thought, as he flailed about screaming the name over and over.

She squeezed his left hand. "Easy, Ken."

His crazed gaze riveted to her. "Lisa?"

Not knowing what else to do, she nodded.

He started to lie back down then jerked up, his face twisted with pain. "Brianne! Where's Brianne?"

"She's okay," Lou lied. "Please, Ken, relax so they can help you. We want you to be okay too."

He nodded and lay back down. He closed his eyes. The attendant replaced the oxygen mask.

"Ken?"

No answer.

"He's unconscious again, ma'am. But his vitals are stable. Just keep talking to him if he wakes up. We need him to be still."

Lou's brain raced. Who attacked Ken and why? Who was Lisa? Brianne? His family?

Good job, Louise, she inwardly scolded. Not only had she fallen in love with a man with a family, she had fallen for someone somebody wanted to kill.

* * *

Steve strode down the polished floors and looked for room 312. He didn't like the antiseptic smell. It brought back memories of wounded soldiers in Korea. Down the hall, Lou leaned against a wall. She looked like hell. Her hair was stringy and snarled from the rain. Dark circles accented her eyes.

"Lou? Are you all right?"

She nodded.

"How's Wiseass?"

She managed a weak smile. "They're letting him rest at the moment. Other than a concussion, three fractured ribs, and a severely dislocated elbow . . ." She choked on the last word and buried her face in her hands.

Steve pulled her into his arms and let her sob. This was one lady who seldom cried and her tears disturbed him.

She sniffed and looked up at him. "That man wanted to *kill* him, Steve! If I hadn't come along . . ." She sobbed into his shirt again.

"Sh! Easy now. Ken will to be all right. I do need to ask you some questions, though. Are you up for that?"

She sniffed again and pulled away. He gave her his hanky. After she completed a healthy nose blowing, he asked, "Did you get a look at the guy?"

She shrugged. "He was tall, about your height. Broad shoulders. His hair was dark. Short." She paused, as if trying to reconstruct that terrible moment. "He had high cheekbones, like a native."

"An Indian? What was he wearing?" Steve asked.

She shrugged. "A T-shirt. Jean jacket, I think."

"What made you think he wanted to kill Ken?"

"Look at what he did to him before I got there. And he had this, this look on his face."

"You said it was dark, remember? How could you tell what the guy was thinking? And he took off the moment you got there. Probably it was just a random robbery and the guy got pissed off when Ken put up a fight." Steve touched the bandage on his forehead. "And Ken does know how to put up a fight. Don't worry; we'll get him. I'll take Sam and head out to the reservation tonight."

The door opened and Dr. Weathers came out, his glasses perched on the lower end of his nose. "I think it's time to wake him up again. You should be there, Louise. How about you, Sheriff? I suppose you have a few questions for him?"

Steve nodded and followed them into the room. Ken lay still on the white sheets. A purplish bruise extended down left his cheek. His right arm was encased in cotton and tensor bandages. Maybe Lou was right. This was a hell of a beating for a simple robbery.

The doctor motioned for Lou to go ahead. She leaned over the bed. "Ken?" she whispered as she gently squeezed his left hand. "Ken?"

Steve noticed the concern on Lou's face. Damn it, he thought. She's fallen for the fellow.

Ken's eyes opened. He blinked, then focused on Steve at the bottom of the bed.

"Hello, Wiseass," Steve said.

"Nice to see you too, Sheriff." Ken turned his head to look at Lou. "You okay?"

Lou nodded and smiled.

Damn, Steve thought as he watched the two of them. This flame won't die easily.

"Tell me what you remember," Steve said. He wanted to interrupt the unspoken conversation going on in the room.

Ken shrugged, then winced. "Not too much, I'm afraid."

"Did you know your attacker?"

Ken shook his head.

"What did he look like?"

"He was big for an Asian."

Lou leaned over the bed. "He didn't look Asian to me, Ken. He looked native. What made you think he was Asian?"

Ken frowned. "I don't know." He shrugged. "It was dark."

Steve guessed Ken probably didn't get a good look at the guy. "Was he trying to rob you?"

Ken shook his head. "I don't remember him saying anything. It happened pretty fast." Ken paused. "How's your head?"

Steve fingered the stitches on his temple. "Fine. Yours is going to be a lot prettier."

Ken grinned then winced.

Dr. Weathers made for the door. "Ten minutes folks, then he should rest."

Ken asked, "When can I leave, Doc?"

"You have a concussion. And broken ribs. You'd best rest here for the night. I'll be back. Ten minutes," he repeated.

Ken rubbed his head.

Lou asked, "Do you need more medication?"

Ken looked at Lou, "I need to get out of here."

"Why?" Steve jabbed the question and at the same time ducked Lou's glare. Lordy, the woman was getting protective.

"There's something I have to do," Ken said.

"What?" Steve asked.

Ken stared at Steve a long moment before he responded, "I don't know. But it's important."

A nurse came in. "Dr. Weathers instructed me to clear the room. Mr. O'Neil needs his rest."

"I'm not leaving," Lou said.

Steve grabbed her arm. "Can I have a word with you?" he hissed into her ear.

Lou came outside with him but she had that damn stubborn tilt to her chin that he knew only too well.

"This guy is a nut case. I don't think you should be alone with him."

"What you think, dear Steve, is irrelevant. Why don't you get back to work and catch the son-of-a-bitch who did this?"

Steve sighed. "Sometimes I wonder how Ted ever put up with you."

Then Lou gave him that damnably charming smile. "I know. He sometimes wondered that as well."

"Shouldn't you at least call Matt?"

Lou shook her head. "Matt's been working around the clock at the grocery store in New Lesbon. I don't want to wake him or his roommate up. I'll call him tomorrow." She patted Steve's arm. "Thanks for caring. Let me know when you catch the bad guy." She kissed his cheek and went back into the room.

Steve quickly headed toward the elevator. He wanted to get away from that damnable smell. Catch the bad guy, Lou had said.

Well, how could she be certain the bad guy wasn't the one in that hospital bed?

TWENTY

October 25, 1962.

Ken blinked in the dim light. The cracked face of his watch told him it was Six-thirty-five. The stabbing pain in his side chased sleep away. Something moved beside his left leg: Lou had fallen asleep in the chair, her head on her forearms.

She had saved his life. He had no doubt about that. But who had tried to kill him? Why had that man attacked him? And why had he thought the man was Asian? Something tugged at his memory. He felt close, so close to remembering.

Something important. *Very* important.

He stroked Lou's hair. It was soft and wavy from the rain the night before.

She stirred and blinked at him. "Hi!"

"Hi, yourself."

"How do you feel?" she asked as she rubbed her neck.

He tried to keep the anxiety out of his voice. "I want to go home. Find my clothes for me, will you?"

She straightened up. "Is that wise?"

He nodded and swung his legs over the side. He suppressed the pain that coursed through his body.

She looked skeptical. "I'm going to check with Dr. Weathers."

"No." He grabbed her wrist. "I'm leaving, Lou. With or without the doctor's blessing. With or without your help."

She locked her eyes onto his. After a moment, she asked, "Who's Lisa?"

Lisa? He thought a moment, then shook his head. "I don't know. Why?"

She nodded. "Okay, I'll ask again later. I'll help you leave on one condition: you come to my place. They've been waking you up every two hours. I can do that."

"Why?"

"It's one way to tell if you begin to bleed inside your skull. If that happens you could lapse into a coma from pressure on the brain. Do we have a deal?"

"Deal," he said.

By the time they got Frank the cabbie out of bed and coerced him to drive them to Lou's, Ken was exhausted. She helped him up the stairs and put him in Matt's bed. It was firmer than hers, she told him, and besides, they would both sleep better in separate beds. He suspected another reason, but did not have the energy to explore the issue. Most likely he would not have liked the answer. She was too smart to be involved with such a weirdo. In spite of his pain, physical and emotional, sleep fuzzed his mind as she covered him up.

"Lou?"

"I'm here."

He wanted to say so much more but could only come up with, "Thanks."

He didn't hear her response.

* * *

Ko looked up at the clear sky that challenged the radio's forecast for precipitation. The temperature had dropped considerably over night and it felt almost too cold to rain.

His eyes landed on the farmer's truck. As he planned to take it to the airfield, he should make sure it was drivable and fueled. The keys were in the ignition, so he didn't have to hot-wire it. It started with the first turn of the key. The fuel gage indicated the tank was half-full.

He noticed a number of empty beer bottles in the back that might rattle at an inopportune time. He got out and began to toss them out. He reached under the seat. Two more bottles hid there along with . . . his fingers closed around a cool narrow tube. He pulled on it, but it was too long to pull out. He then felt under the front seat, found it again. This time it came out easily.

A rifle. Of what caliber, he did not know. He was not familiar with guns of this vintage. But he had enough experience to know the clip was missing. Another search under the seat revealed nothing. He looked at the dashboard. There, in front of the passenger side in the dash, he saw the outline of a drawer. There was no handle. It took him a minute to realize he had to compress the button on the front to get the door to lower. Inside he was rewarded with a clip of bullets. Six. He slid the clip on the weapon.

He aimed at a branch several yards away. The bullet bit into the branch to the left of where he had aimed. The sights were off, but not by much. He replaced the weapon under the seat. He would not need it to kill O'Neil. But it would come in handy after his mission was accomplished.

Now to plan the ambush. With the newly risen sun at his back, he broke into a jog. When he reached the tracks, he sprang up the embankment and turned left. There, the more level terrain allowed him to set a steady cadence.

In spite of the cold air, his quick pace caused him to perspire. The cuts on his thighs began to sting and he welcomed the discomfort.

Nine miles later, he came to an intersection where another set of tracks angled off. He turned northward and followed the rail line that now paralleled a major connector. He kept his ears tuned, ready to bolt for the bushes if he detected an approaching vehicle.

Twenty minutes later the crest of Chinaman Bluff loomed to his left. He smiled at the irony of the name. He left the tracks and turned up the narrow road that he knew led to Volk Airfield. His pace slowed as his eyes searched the trees on each side.

Within a hundred yards, he found what he was looking for - an opening in the brush that would provide the perfect spot for his ambush.

He studied the area and memorized the shapes of trees and bushes so he would be able to locate the exact that night. On his way home he turned off at the base of the bluff and followed a faint winding trail up the steep incline.

There was little evidence that humans had used this trail recently. He slowed to a walk as the steepness increased. At times he had to scramble; at others, he was forced to climb over boulders. Finally he reached the spot he was looking for. Below him row upon row of stationary bombers lined the tarmac, armed and at the ready.

The sun topped the bluff and reflected off the wings of the planes. He would return here after he disposed of O'Neil and watch the planes take off. Friendly fire would occur over the Atlantic. Nuclear war would result. History would unfold as it should.

Then, after allowing himself a moment to remember Shimira, he would use the farmer's rifle one last time.

* * *

Lou woke up with a start. The clock confirmed her fears. It was nearly ten. So much for waking Ken up every two hours.

She sprinted to Matt's room and remembered at the last minute to grab her robe. The nightdress she had on was a favorite of hers, only it was so old and had been washed so often that the flannel was nearly transparent. Though why she was suddenly shy she wasn't sure. Probably because of Lisa, whoever she was.

Ken's breathing was so shallow she had to lean over him to detect it. But it was regular and his features were relaxed. She stole out of the room and down to the phone in the kitchen.

Alice answered on the second ring. "Mauston Public School, may I help you?"

"Hi, Alice."

"Louise! The sheriff called and said you and Ken wouldn't be in today. Apparently Ken was mugged last night and is in the hospital. Is everything all right?" Alice's words flowed without a pause for breath and Louise wondered if the secretary had been an opera singer in a former life.

"We're fine." She didn't divulge she was home and had Ken upstairs. "I'll call later and let you know if either of us will be in tomorrow. I suspect I will be but Ken might need the rest of the week off."

"I'll pass this along to Principal Wilson. Take care, dear."

As soon as Lou hung up, she checked her watch again. Although she did want to talk to Matt before the rumors spread to New Lesbon, he would already be back at the store. She decided to try to call him after supper. She went back up to check on Ken. Time for a reality check, if that was possible with this fellow.

She sat beside Ken on the bed and nudged him gently. He stirred a little and muttered something. After another nudge, his eyes opened part way and he smiled.

"Good morning."

"Good morning to you, sir," she responded. "Who are you?"

"Ken. Ken O'Neil. Beat up history teacher."

"And who is your wife?"

He frowned up at her. "I don't have one."

She sat down beside him. "Last night in the ambulance, you called out two names. Lisa and Brianne." She watched him closely but he only looked puzzled, then increasingly frustrated.

He sighed, "That just doesn't make any sense."

"Tell me about it."

She stood as he awkwardly swung his legs over the edge, then she sat down beside him once more.

He studied her a moment, then said, "Why on earth would you let a crazy man stay in your house?"

She shrugged. "If you come up with a good answer to that I'd appreciate you sharing it before Steve asks me the same question."

He smiled and looked around the room. "Well, you can tell him with all honesty that I slept in Matt's room." He looked at his watch. "We're late for school."

"I phoned in. Steve had already been in contact with them. We've been excused for the day and I told them you might need the rest of the week off."

Ken struggled to his feet and walked over to Matt's workstation. He glanced over the few sketches on the desktop. "Wow, your son is talented."

Wanting to cling to a safe subject, Lou prompted, "Want to see what he's done?"

"I do."

She opened the curtains to the morning light, then pulled out a stack of paintings and set them onto the bed. She lifted one at a time for him to see. She did not try to hide the pride she felt as Ken exclaimed over each one.

But she was not prepared for his reaction when she came to the early sketch Matt had done of her. Ken sank to his knees and his breathing grew ragged.

"Ken, what is it?"

His eyes remained riveted to the sketch on the bed. He reached out and touched it. His hand began to shake.

"Ken, what is it?"

He pointed at the picture. "That's-that's Lisa." His voice was rough, broken.

She knelt beside him. Finally, some answers. "Who's Lisa?"

His face twisted with grief. "My wife."

"Where is she?" she whispered.

"Dead." The word came out with a gush of air.

Guilt coursed through her at the relief Lou felt. Determined to help him remember, she asked, "And Brianne?"

"My daughter." He choked out, "Oh, God." He breathed unevenly, clutched his side, then said, "I remember…"

She held her own breath, afraid if she said anything, he might stop talking.

"It was a terrorist attack in the mall. A bomb. They died along with thirty others. Three years ago."

He blinked through them at her. "You look a bit like her."

Stung, she back. "Is that why you were attracted to me? You were subconsciously looking for a substitute for your wife?"

He reached out and touched her arm. "No, no. I had no memory of Lisa when we met. You looked familiar, but that wasn't why I wanted to get to know you." He looked at the brace on her wrist. "It was that, actually."

She started. "My brace?"

"Yeah. You lost your husband, raised Matt by yourself. The accident took away your art. Yet . . . you pulled through." He touched her cheek. "That light you have in you, your strength. That's what drew me to you."

Then his features froze and he looked about him. "Oh Jesus." His left hand flew to his forehead. "Oh, Jesus." His breathing grew ragged.

"Ken?"

He didn't answer. His eyes squeezed shut as if trying to block out what he was saw in his mind.

She kneeled in front of him. "Ken, what is it?"

He sat back onto the floor and opened his eyes. She had never seen so much dread in a person's expression. He blinked at her then rose awkwardly to his feet. He began to slowly pace the room. His eyes darted here and there without focusing on anything.

She couldn't stand it any longer. She blocked his path. "What are you remembering?"

He stared at her. "What's today?" he demanded.

"Thursday."

"The date!"

"October 25th."

He swung his left arm up to his face and blinked at his watch, looked out the window, and then back at his watch. He rubbed his face with his left hand. Then he looked her up and down, frowned, and glanced out the door toward her bedroom. He paled. "Oh, Jesus, what have I done?"

"What?" Would he ever make sense?

"What if – what if I got you pregnant?"

Shock rode through her, followed quickly by a tide of anger. If that was all he was worried about . . . She took two steps back. "Don't trouble yourself. I'm not asking for any commitment here. In fact you can leave. Right now." She turned and flew down the stairs.

"Wait! You don't understand."

She understood all right. He regretted what they had done the night before. End of story. She switched on the radio and turned the volume up in an effort to drown out his words.

Someone pounded heavily on the door. A peek through the window revealed Steve's car out front. Still ignoring Ken, she went to the front door and flung it open. For once, Steve's meddling was about to come in handy.

"I just checked at the hospital . . ." His blue eyes riveted to Ken. "What the hell is *he* doing here?"

"He was just leaving."

Steve blinked at her. "Geez, Lou, are you all right?"

"No!"

He glared at Ken. "Did that sonofa—?"

The radio blared for attention. "We interrupt our current program to bring you this urgent announcement."

"DEFCON Two," Ken announced bitterly.

The radio announcer continued, "The pentagon has just announced that the military remains at DEFCON 2 Alert status, one step away from nuclear war."

Steve turned back around. "How did you . . .?"

Lou realized at the same time as Steve that Ken had gone.

Without a word.

"Lou?" Steve managed to pierce her bewilderment.

She was hurt and angry and directed her ire at the nearest target. She shoved Steve out the door. "Why don't you just drop the questions and go play sheriff? I can take care of myself." She shut the door on his surprised expression.

Lou felt a little calmer after her outburst. She snuck a peak through the curtain. Steve walked away, shaking his head. No doubt he thought she was crazy as well.

Then the tears came.

Tears of fear for Matt, and for the future he might never have.

Tears for the charming Ken she had fallen in love with and who had been replaced by a cold, bitter person.

A person who regretted making love to her.

TWENTY-ONE

When Ken opened the front door he could hear Mrs. Lacey tapping away at the typewriter. He stole up the stairs and past her door to the bathroom. He now recognized the man in the mirror. Just before he entered the time chamber they had cut his hair to the shorter style worn by men in the 1960's and given him a sport jacket with a fake birth certificate and cash sewn into the lining. When the lining ripped during his rescue attempt, the river had stolen the cash.

He needed to rest if he had any hope of doing what he had to do that night. And for that he needed something to dull the dueling pains in his side and elbow. He foraged through the medicine cabinet for anything that looked like a painkiller. Finally he saw something that looked familiar. A small tin with 'Aspirin' in red letters across the front.

He placed his thumb's nail in the little dent and tried to pry it open. The tiny lid wouldn't budge. Surely he wasn't *that* weak. He transferred it to his right hand, which, because of his splinted elbow, stuck out two feet from his body. When he again tried to pry open the lid, his arm throbbed in protest and he had to suppress an oath.

He turned on the light above the sink and turned the tin over. Two small red triangles pointed to the back edge. "Squeeze here" it read.

"What the hell," he muttered. Using two hands he squeezed. The front of the tin popped open.

Shaking with relief, he fully opened the lid. Inside were six white tablets. He popped all of them into his mouth and used his left hand to cup water to wash them down. Hopefully, they would dull the ache enough to allow him a few hours of sleep. He needed the rest if he ever hoped to accomplish what he had to do.

He returned to his room. *His room* – not for long. He opened the French doors a crack removed his shoes, and sat upon the bed. The cool breeze smelled clean after the rain of the night before. He lay on top of the quilts, not bothering to even take his shoes off. After a short nap he would say good-bye to the nice lady who had taken a stranger into her home.

He realized then just how lucky he'd been since arriving in 1962. All the good people who had helped him: Sergeant Stevens, Mrs. Lacey, Mrs. Wilson, Lou.

Painful memories filled his head. In the fall of 2044, wanting control of New America's land and water, China had initiated an air and sea blockade. This led to the collapse of the newly opened stock market. Private enterprise strangled. The crime rate increased. Within three years his country withered from burgeoning prosperity to destitution. Lisa and Brianne were killed while shopping for a birthday present for him.

In 2047, Ito Nishimura, a Japanese scientist who had recently defected to New America, approached the government with an absurd proposition: Use his adaptation of teleportation technology to send someone back in time to prevent the 'mistake' in 1962 that led to war.

Two years of collaboration with American scientists yielded blueprints for time chambers. Ken's exchange subject from 1962 had been an alcoholic who had lost his job and his wife after mistreating both in favor of the bottle. Research showed that on the evening of August 5th, 1962 he had driven off the bridge in Wausau, Wisconsin. The body was never found.

Ken, who had published articles on the Nuclear Conflict of '62, had been called in to advise Lieutenant Peter Michaels to prepare him for the journey. But Michaels had died and the imminent attack on the bunker had left the Americans no choice but to send Ken.

They were supposed to destroy the time chambers immediately after they sent him here. But, as the Chinese had managed to transport an agent to 1962 as well, they must have prevented the Americans from doing that. And if Ken hadn't taught top-level kickboxing, last night would have turned out a lot differently.

One thing was certain: If Ken didn't stop the planes from taking off tonight, nuclear war would result.

His original plan had been to jog to Volk Airfield and be there when the alarms went off. Now he would have to leave hours earlier, as in his current condition, he could only achieve a walk. And every step along the way he would have to watch his back.

He should have a weapon of sorts, but where could he purchase such a thing? He had never fired a gun at another person. Would he be able to, if it came to that?

Sleep began to wedge into his crammed consciousness and he opened a path for it. He would need all the rest he could get if he had any hope at all of evading the Chinese agent and preventing those planes from taking off.

* * *

Lou did what she always did when upset: clean. With Matt away most of the time, things weren't that bad, and by one o'clock in the afternoon the entire house had been given the once over. She showered, dressed, and after a sandwich, pedaled to the school, intent on getting on with her life – without Ken O'Neil.

She ignored the curious glances and dismissed Miss Ingram who had come in to spare for her. When the others asked about Ken, they all got the same answer: "I wouldn't know."

She decided to stay and mark the essays in her classroom instead of taking them home as she usually did. This way the loneliness at home would be postponed. And by the time she got there, perhaps sleep could rescue her before she could think too much.

"You're working late."

She looked up to see Principal Wilson peering over reading glasses perched on the bridge of her nose.

Lou glanced at her watch; five forty-five. "And you," she replied.

Mrs. Wilson came in, perched on the edge of the desk, and narrowed her eyes at Lou.

Lou met her gaze as evenly as she could, then said, "What?"

"You know I've better things to do than collect gossip. But when I fear for the well-being of one of my teachers I feel obliged to step in where I wouldn't normally."

Lou gave her best shot at a smile but knew the alert hazel eyes noticed the hesitancy. Tears swelled behind her lids but she refused to allow them to flow. Ken had called her strong. And she was. She could move past this.

"I am fine," she lied.

"You are not," Mrs. Wilson defied, but quickly added, "Any distress you may be experiencing because of Mr. O'Neil will weigh heavily on my conscience. I would shudder to think my judgment of him was not accurate and that he may have brought harm to anyone here, student or teacher."

"No, Ken's a good man. He wouldn't hurt anyone." Lou bit her lip. Why was she so quick to defend him? She thought a moment. Ken *was* a good man. Whoever he was. At least he had been before he remembered what happened to his family. And she knew, all too well, how family tragedy could change a person. He may have regretted their intimacy but she was still convinced he was not a bad person.

She sought Mrs. Wilson's gaze and held it. "He did me no harm. Why would you think he had?"

Mrs. Wilson presented one of her rare smiles. "I don't gossip, but I never claimed not to listen. Several of the staff commented on how you responded when they asked about him."

"We've had a-a falling out. I think I'm just getting too old for this dating thing."

"Nonsense. One is never too old. I was concerned your anger might have been caused by some improper behavior on his part."

Lou shook her head. No doubt rumors about Ken spending the night at her place had animated the town's chat line. "No. He's a gentleman." A bit weird, but a gentleman.

"Then may I ask how he is? Will I expect him to return tomorrow?"

Lou shook her head and answered honestly. "I really don't know. He has a few cracked ribs and a dislocated right elbow, so I think he could teach but . . ." She thought of his anguished response when he remembered the loss of his family.

"But?" Mrs. Wilson prodded. "Sometimes a mugging of this sort leaves an emotional scar. He is welcome to take what time he needs to recover."

Lou knew whatever she told the principal would be kept in confidence. She sighed. "He has regained some of his memory and what he remembers is rather tragic. I'm not sure what his immediate plans are other than I am not part of them."

Mrs. Wilson's gaze softened. "With all this talk of nuclear attack, who knows what the next few days will bring on a global scale, let alone a personal one. Things might not be as bad as they seem." She stood up. "Let me know if you need time off, or extra work, whatever will help the most."

"Thanks, I will."

"Now, go home, so I can. I hate to see someone put more hours into this place than I do."

Lou stacked the papers. "I doubt that happens very often."

"Good-night." Mrs. Wilson walked out of the room with the erect posture of a general.

Lou gathered up her things and peered outside. It was time she got home.

After last night, she did not want to be alone on the streets after dark.

TWENTY-TWO

A sharp pain in his right elbow jolted Ken awake. In a panic he looked at his watch, then relaxed. It was just past five o'clock. Six hours to get to Volk Field. Should be enough, even in his current state.

When he moved, several parts of his body complained fiercely and he worried the pain might not subside.

He caught his image in the bureau's mirror. His right arm stuck out from his side. When he removed the splint he was afraid it would dangle uselessly like a broken wing. But the elbow was swollen and rigor-mortis stiff. Any attempt to bend it resulted in pain raking from his fingers to his shoulder.

The stairs creaked a greeting – or was it a farewell? – under his feet as he made his way down to the kitchen. It was only when he reached the bottom that the silence registered. No tapping of typewriter keys.

The light was on in the kitchen. Mrs. Lacey tossed him a smile as she spooned soup into a bowl.

"Have a seat, dear," she said.

He sat down. When she turned back to him her eyes gleamed. With sadness? Perhaps. But also with something else.

"I've cooked supper – can you believe it?" She set a steaming bowl in front of him. "Well," she added humbly, "Mr. Campbell helped me with the soup. But I made chicken sandwiches like you make them, with mayonnaise and lettuce. I wanted you to have a nice meal to help you get your strength back."

To his dismay, he felt tears threaten. "I have to leave," he blurted.

She sat down across from him and patted his hand. "I know. Eat up."

He stared at her.

She shrugged. "I'm no Einstein, but I knew once your memory returned there would be things you had to do."

If you only knew, he thought. "How did you know I got my memory back?"

She reached across the table and patted his hand. "I looked in on you while you slept. I could tell by the sadness on your face. And it's still there. Good Lord, Kenneth, it looks as if someone has stolen your smile. From your face, from your eyes, and . . . from your heart?"

He sighed in an attempt to keep from breaking down. What kind of a soft noodle had he become? He focused on what he wanted to say.

"I-I really appreciate everything you have done for me."

Her loud laugh startled him. She actually threw her head back to allow the sound to come out.

"The scales are very unbalanced here. Don't you realize what you've done for me?"

She got up from the table and pulled a large envelope from the drawer behind her. She pulled out a letter, then set it beside his plate before she resumed her seat. "Now, read that. But eat first."

He nibbled at a wedge of sandwich while he read the letter. It was a manuscript acceptance from Brooks Publishing in New York.

Mrs. Lacey beamed. "And I've gotten another one since then. They want more of my stories, can you imagine that?"

He nodded. "Well, yes I can."

"And they sent me a nice check. I'll be able to hire someone to keep this place up to snuff. I'm even thinking of getting in a maid. Isn't that a hoot?"

"Congratulations." He tried to keep the word from sounding hollow. He really was glad to see her succeeding at what she obviously loved doing.

Outside the sun had set. He stood up. "I really have to get going." He hesitated. "Could I ask a favor of you?"

"Anything, dear."

"Would you phone Mrs. Wilson and let her know I won't be returning to teach? Tell her – tell her how much I appreciated the job."

Mrs. Lacey patted his left arm. "Don't you worry. I'll call Irma first thing in the morning. They have good teachers there, they'll manage." She looked up at him, her face wrinkled with worry. "That man who attacked you, do you know him?"

He sighed and shook his head. "I've never seen him before." It wasn't a lie.

"Is there a chance he could attack you again?"

He hesitated, then blurted, "I don't suppose Mr. Lacey owned a gun I could borrow?" He gave himself a mental kick. Why had he asked her that? It would only make her worry.

But her head bobbed with enthusiasm. "Wait here," she ordered and went up the stairs faster than Ken would have thought possible.

She came down with something out of an old Western film. A Colt 45. "My husband kept this in his night table. After he passed on I brought it into my room. Some of his paranoia rubbed off I guess. Quite a bit actually," she confessed. "But that has eased since you came along."

The gun felt heavy in his hand. "Look, I . . ."

She wagged an index finger at him. "Take it. Just be careful. I don't want you shooting your foot, or worse, taking an eye out. Not one of those beautiful eyes."

"Thanks." For trusting him with a gun, no less. And for not asking more questions.

He reached into the closet for his suit coat.

"Oh, don't you have anything warmer than that? It's nippy out there. It feels as if it could snow."

"Don't worry, I'll buy something."

"Nothing will be open this time of night. You wait right here."

With déjà vu he watched her race up the stairs again. She returned with what looked like a relic from World War Two. Which, he quickly decided, really wasn't that long ago. It was a short-waisted leather jacket with fur around the narrow collar. "US Navy" was embroidered on the front pocket. The dark-brown leather was soft, supple, unmarred. It looked new.

"I can't —" he began, but she shushed him.

"My husband got that when he retired. He hardly wore it. He wasn't much for going out. I want you to have it."

Ken could not disappoint her by turning it down. "Thanks." That word hardly did the job but he didn't know what else to say. He slid his stiff right arm in first, then slid on the rest of the jacket. It was a little bulky, but the sleeves were perfect. When he tucked the Colt into the side of his waistband and zipped the jacket shut, no one would be able to tell he was armed.

"Looks good." Mrs. Lacey adjusted the collar a little and he could see tears misting in her eyes.

He kissed her forehead and smiled down at her.

Her eyes brightened. "There, your smile wasn't stolen after all. Don't keep it hidden, Kenneth. It's too nice a smile, especially when you use your eyes."

This caused him to smile again, although it brought tears dangerously close to the surface. "I'd better go."

She nodded. "When it's all over, I'd love to hear your story. I bet it's a grand tale."

Oh yes, he thought, as he walked away into the night. A grand tale, indeed. But not one he could ever share with anyone.

The cold night wind bit into his face and he was grateful for the jacket. He kept to the shadows and constantly looked behind him. Thank God for the gun. If the agent came after him now, he'd need it.

After he passed the park a thought came to him. Was the gun even loaded? He hid behind the next big tree and after a peek to make sure he was alone, he pulled the gun out, and held it in his left hand. To his relief, all six chambers were filled. He shoved the revolver back inside his belt and walked on. The ache in his elbow subsided, only to be overcome by a stitch in his side that forced him to slow down. Christ, what a mess.

He saw a police car turn the corner and he ducked into an ally until it passed. The last thing he wanted was have a chat with good ol' Steve.

Despair grew within him when he realized he would not be able to walk fast enough to reach Volk Field before midnight. What the hell could he do? Force someone at gunpoint to drive him?

He noticed a phone booth on the corner. Frank. Ken hated to involve the cabbie, but he would tell the fellow to leave as soon as he dropped Ken at the airfield. However, Bessie informed him Frank was not working. The cabbie had closed his business to finish his bomb shelter.

Ken stepped back out into the wind. As a kid rode by on a bicycle an idea came to him. The only person he knew who owned a bicycle was Lou. It would take at least half an hour to get to her place.

On to plan B, he thought. The shadows were deep and long. He appeared to be the only person out and about. Apparently the town's occupants had retired to their warm homes for the evening. The temperature had dropped and Ken's cheeks and right hand tingled with the cold. Yet the effort of walking made him perspire. His fatigue grew and he was relieved when he came to the last corner. But as he turned it, his relief disappeared. He ducked behind a large oak as fast as his ribs allowed.

Sheriff Jensen's squad car slowed to a halt and parked in front of Lou's house.

Ken decided it wouldn't be prudent to try to steal Lou's bike while Steve was so close. He rested against the big trunk, thankful to be out of the wind. But the night air soon cooled the moisture inside his shirt and before long he began to shiver.

Hopefully the sheriff's visit would be a short one.

TWENTY-THREE

Steve nestled the tires of his squad car next to the curb and peered through the passenger window. There was a light on in the kitchen. He had been anxious to speak with Lou since the rumor mill began grinding out stories about her break-up with Wiseass. That was one thing about a small town. Someone couldn't sneeze funny without another person hearing it and telling someone else about it.

Steve grabbed the bag of doughnuts he had just picked up at the bakery and headed for the house. He and Lou usually did this in the middle of the morning on school holidays. He would bring the doughnuts and Lou would supply the coffee. Fifteen minutes of snack and chat then back to work.

He rapped lightly on the door. Lou answered with a smile that was not convincing. Without a word, she went over to the stove and proceeded to fill a mug with coffee.

He set the doughnuts on the table and pulled up the chair. "These are still warm. Fred was sugaring them just as I arrived. He wanted to sell me the morning ones and I said, no way, Jose."

She gave him another wan smile as she set the mug in front of him. His stomach rumbled in anticipation at the bittersweet aromas of coffee and fresh doughnuts. He studied Lou as she sat down opposite him and sipped in silence. When she reached for a doughnut he knew he would have to initiate the conversation.

He also picked up a doughnut. "So, when are you going to apologize?" he asked. The best way to get Lou to open up was to irk her.

Her eyebrows shot up. "Apologize? For what?"

He nodded as he chewed. After swallowing he said, "For telling me to go play sheriff."

She licked sugar off her fingertips. "Oh yeah. Sorry."

He sighed in frustration. The very fact she did not venture anything further only proved something bad had gone down. He reined in his mounting impatience and tried another approach, one sure to piss her off.

"It wasn't a good idea bringing that nut here from the hospital. What are the neighbors going to think, with him being here alone with you? What kind of a reputation are you going for?"

Her eyes flashed and he knew he had a base hit.

"First of all, Ken may be a bit crazy, but he is not dangerous. And secondly, it was officially morning when we got here from the hospital." Her words kept pace with her temper. "And thirdly, I don't give a rat's ass what you or the neighbors think. If I want a man here, I'll have him whenever and for however long I want."

She stood up, stomped to the sink, dumped her coffee down the drain, and then faced him with folded arms. The coffee break was over.

He reached for another doughnut and chewed slowly. "Ummph, these are good."

"Time to go, Steve."

He shook his head, swallowed, then said, "I'm not ready to play sheriff."

"Well I don't need you to play big brother either."

"Oh yes you do – when you've fallen so hard for a nutcase who doesn't even know who the hell he is."

He feared she would throw something at him. But instead she said, with a stone face and matching tone, "He does remember who he is and it's over between us. So go catch yourself some jaywalkers, big brother."

"Ouch." Her sarcasm could cut mighty fine at times. "Why is it over?"

She sighed. "Does it matter?"

He stood up and walked over to her. "Yes. Because if that son of a bitch did anything out of line . . . "

"He did nothing I didn't want him to." Her green eyes were steady, but he noticed moisture creeping in at the edges.

Ken *had* hurt her. And it made Steve want to use the fellow as a punching bag. "Is there anything I can do?"

She smiled, more naturally this time. "Take the rest of those doughnuts home. They're delicious and if they're here in the morning, I'll eat them instead of a healthy breakfast."

"Okeydokey."

He picked up his mug and slurped the dregs. She did make great coffee. Susan's didn't taste as good, even though she had tried to mimic Lou's technique.

Lou re-rolled the top of the doughnut bag and handed it to him on his way to the door. "Any news about the man who attacked Ken?"

Steve shook his head. "None. The chief out at the reservation had no idea. And you know how I hate mysteries. That's why I'm cruisin' tonight instead of at home watching "I Love Lucy" with Susan."

Before he left she laid a hand on his arm. "Thanks."

"Anytime, kid." He used to call Ted that and Lou had acquired the address shortly after moving to Mauston.

He revved the engine, then with a final wave, drove off. He was relieved about the break-up but he hated to see Lou hurtin' that way.

She sure had fallen hard.

* * *

Lou got the operator to connect her to the number in New Lesbon that Matt had given her.

"Hey Mom," Matt's voice sounded thick.

"Oh, did I wake you, honey?"

"Yeah, but that's okay. Joe and I were watching a movie and I fell asleep." His voice cleared with tension. "Is everything okay?"

So he hadn't heard anything yet. She briefly described the events of the night before as an attempted robbery, as that's most likely what it was.

"Jesus, is Ken okay?"

Lou sighed at his oath, but was too weary to argue the point. "He spent the night in the hospital, but he's back at Mrs. Lacey's now." She didn't tell him anything else. That could wait until the weekend. "When are you coming home?"

"I have to work Saturday but I'm catching the bus to Mauston right after work. It should get in around eight. I'll bring those groceries I put away for you."

"That sounds great," Lou said.

"Is everything okay, Mom? You don't sound so good."

"I'm just tired, thanks." She knew she would spill her guts and probably a few tears come Saturday night. She never could keep anything that bothered her from Matt for very long.

"See you Saturday, Mom."

"I'll keep supper warm for you."

A cold emptiness filled the house as Lou went up the stairs. Come morning, she'd probably have to turn the radiators on. She removed her dress and nylons and donned stretch slacks and a comfy turtleneck.

Before she headed down the stairs, she went into Matt's room. She pulled out that earlier sketch Matt had done of her. No, she decided, it didn't really look like her. But apparently it looked enough like Lisa to awaken Ken's memory.

She put the painting back into the stack and looked out the window, half expecting to see snow. The maple tree, stripped of its leaves by recent fall breezes, eerily guarded the empty yard. Movement in the alley caught her eye. A man hunched over against the cold pushed a bicycle. In the dim light she couldn't see any of his features except for the leather jacket the fellow wore. The jacket did not look familiar, but she did recognize the bicycle.

"Son of a bitch!" she yelled as she bounded down the stairs. That bicycle was her only means of transportation and by God no one was going to just walk away with it. An inner voice warned her to call Steve, but the perpetrator certainly wasn't Ken's attacker and she intended to give whoever it was one hell of a tongue-lashing once she caught up to him.

He was halfway down the next street by the time she got to the end of the alley.

"Hey!" she hollered.

The man didn't look back, but mounted her bicycle.

She broke into a sprint, knowing that she would never be able to catch him once he started pedaling. But the fellow no sooner got both feet on the pedals when he keeled over onto the macadam. He began to writhe and moan.

She recognized the voice and closed the short distance.

Ken looked up at her, his features twisted into a grimace. He gritted his teeth, took a short breath, and said, "Oh hi, Lou," in a casual tone that belied the pain in his eyes.

"Ken? What the hell are you doing?"

She offered her hand and he leaned heavily on her as he struggled to his feet. He looked on the verge of vomiting when he faced her.

"C-Can I borrow your bike?" Violent shivers made him stutter.

"No." She wanted to stay angry. She picked up her bicycle and began to wheel it back. The brisk air penetrated the loose wool of her sweater and she, too started to shiver.

"Please!"

She stopped and looked back at him. He hesitantly took a few steps toward her. The intensity in his eyes matched that of his plea. His shivering obviously made his pain worse.

What resolve she had, fled. "Come on," she said. "Let's go inside where it's warm."

By the time she parked her bicycle behind the gate, he had managed to climb the steps.

Once inside, she motioned to a chair next to the living room radiator. "Sit here." She turned the knob and the responding creaks assured her heat would soon come. He still shivered, even though he still had his jacket on.

"Nice jacket."

He nodded. "Mr. L-Lacey's."

"Oh, did you steal that too?"

His eyes flashed black anger, then dulled with pain. "I-I am not a th-thief."

She pulled an afghan off the sofa and wrapped it around his shoulders.

"Th-thanks."

"So, you were only borrowing my bicycle?"

He nodded. His breathing slowed and the shivering subsided. His eyes regained their power and Lou tried to stare him down.

"What for?" she demanded.

"I have to get to Volk Field before Midnight."

"Why?"

"It's important."

"If it's so important why didn't you borrow Mr. Lacey's car and drive there yourself?"

"I don't know how to drive. Before last night I could have run there, but I'm no longer able to do that."

"Well, it doesn't look as if you're able to ride a bike either. You do know how to ride a bicycle, don't you?"

Heat poured off the radiator. No longer shivering, he pulled off the afghan. "You made it look easy." His eyes locked onto hers. "Will you teach me?"

"Why should I?"

"Because it's important."

"Why?" She flung her hands in exasperation.

Instead of answering, he opened his jacket. She reached over to help him take it off, but recoiled when she saw the gun.

"It's okay," he said softly. "Mrs. Lacey gave it to me. In case I got attacked again."

"Oh, right." For the first time she felt truly frightened of him. "You try to steal my bike. Then I find out you've got a gun. I think I'd better call Steve." She continued to step away as she spoke.

"Why don't you call Mrs. Lacey?"

She pulled up short at that. She thought a moment. "Give me the gun first."

He pulled the gun out by his fingertips, set it gently onto the floor in front of him, then pushed it away with his foot. "Be careful, it's loaded."

She knelt down and reached for it, worried he might make a grab for her. But he didn't move. The metal of the gun felt cold in her hand.

"I'm sorry if I frightened you."

She spun away and headed for the phone on the kitchen counter. Damn him. What was it about his eyes and his voice that made him appear so sincere?

She set the gun on the counter and picked up the phone. Joyce, the teenage daughter of a neighbor, was talking to some boy on the party line.

"Excuse, me, Joyce. This is Louise Jensen. Could I please use the phone? It's important. I won't be long."

When she got the dial tone she dialed Bessie and got Mrs. Lacey's number. Her anxiety rose to its previous level when Mrs. Lacey didn't answer by the fifth ring.

"Let it ring!" Ken yelled from the living room. "She's probably upstairs typing."

"Right." Lou allowed sarcasm into her voice but inwardly hoped Mrs. Lacey would answer. Her throat tightened more with each ring. At twenty she realized she had been holding her breath and let it escape in a rush. Twenty-two. She would hang up at twenty-five and call Steve. Twenty-four. Twenty-five. She hung up.

She turned to find Ken heading to the front door.

She pounded after him. "No, don't you dare leave."

He ignored her and spoke over his shoulder. "I'm taking your bicycle. With or without lessons. I'd prefer to take the gun, but I understand why you don't want me to have it." His voice and expression were both level and controlled. But he could not keep the pain out of his eyes.

She could have tried to stop him and would most likely have succeeded, considering his injuries. But she did not have the heart to hurt him. She was about to plead with him when he opened the door.

Big snowflakes swirled into the doorway. The small lawn was already white.

He sighed. His shoulders slumped.

"Ken, even without the snow, you wouldn't have gotten far on that bicycle, and you know it."

When he turned around his distress was so visible that she wanted to hug him. Then a light crossed his eyes. Ken shut the door behind him and stepped close. "You said you drove before the accident. You could borrow Mr. Lacey's car and drive me to Volk Field."

Paralysis crept over her at the thought of driving. She shook her head and backed up. A snowstorm the night of her accident had rendered the road slick with ice. She couldn't imagine driving on a sunny summer day, let alone at night with it snowing.

"Please, Lou. I *have* to get there!"

"I can't drive. It took me six months to get to the point where I could even sit in a car."

"Jesus, Lou! I need to get there before midnight."

"*Why?* Why is it so important?"

He stared at her a moment. Then he went into the kitchen, sat down at the table, and motioned for her to sit across from him. She joined him, hopeful that finally he tell her everything.

Although she wasn't at all sure if she wanted to hear it.

TWENTY-FOUR

Ko found the spot he had picked out earlier. He backed the truck up off the road as far as the bushes allowed. It was eight o'clock.

He shut the truck off, rolled the window down and breathed the pine-sharpened air into his lungs. At first it was crisp, exhilarating. Then it grew heavier. Over the next hour clouds moved in. Snowflakes, at first sporadic, multiplied and soon covered everything in a lather of white. He rolled the window up except for a small opening so he could hear if a vehicle approached.

The truck's interior soon matched the temperature outside, but he blocked out the cold by concentrating on listening. He would ram the car as it passed in front of him. Then, he would haul O'Neil out of the wreck and dislocate the bones in the teacher's neck. Death would be instantaneous. Nearly painless.

In the unlikely event O'Neil managed to drive by, Ko would use the rifle to disable his car. Then he would grab the American, haul him out, and break his neck.

Different story. Same ending.

* * *

Ken reached across the table and gently cupped Lou's left hand in his. What surprised him was that she let him. Yet her green eyes regarded him with more than a little wariness.

"At midnight tonight, a guard at Duluth Section Direction Center will detect an intruder and sound the sabotage alarm. This will automatically set off all alarms in the surrounding area, including Volk Field. However, the alarm at Volk Field is wired incorrectly. That alarm will order F-106A fighter jets to take off. These planes are armed with nuclear air-to-air missiles. Because the nation is at DEFCON 2, all alert drills have been canceled and the pilots will believe they are at war."

Lou opened her mouth to speak but he held up his hand. "Let me finish. The pilots have not been informed there are other American bombers in the air and do not know their alert routes. Friendly fire will occur over the eastern seaboard of the United States, and Strategic Air Command will assume they are under attack. They will authorize its entire fleet of bombers to prepare for a full-scale attack on the Soviet Union. The Soviets will intercept the message and instruct Cuba to launch its twenty Luna missiles. Both nations will think the other has pre-empted."

"Has what?" Lou asked in an intense whisper.

"Pre-empted. Fired first."

She stared at him, disbelief on her face, in her eyes. "How can you know all this?"

"I'm psychic." He hated lying to her and quickly added, "Sort of." He squeezed her hand. "This will happen, Lou. God knows I would not ask you to go where my attacker could be waiting, but if I don't get to

Volk Field to stop those planes from taking off, you will die anyhow, along with everyone else who lives in the eastern half of this country."

"Who attacked you? Why would he want to stop you?"

"He's a Chinese agent who wants those planes to take off."

"Why?"

"If the Soviet Union and the United States destroy one another, China will emerge as the sole superpower."

Lou leaned back in her chair, as it that would help her focus. "How could your attacker know this? No, let me guess. He's psychic as well?"

He shrugged off her sarcasm and tried to balance on the narrow line of truth. "I don't know."

She frowned. "I don't believe the psychic stuff."

"The psychic part is not important. I *know* what is going to happen: a nuclear conflict that can be prevented if I can get to Volk Field before midnight. Lou, you *have* to drive me there."

She sagged against the back of the chair, her face crumbling in terror. "I just can't. It's not like I haven't tried. Every once in awhile I'll sit behind the wheel in Steve's car. I-I just freeze up. And with it snowing . . . Oh, God." She pulled her hair back from her face and sighed.

Then her face lit up. "What about Frank?"

Ken shook his head. "Frank's not taking calls until he's finished his bomb shelter." He looked at his watch. "I'm running out of time."

Lou pushed her chair back and went to the phone.

Ken got up too quickly and had to sit back down to dampen the fire in his side. "Who are you calling?" he rasped out.

Lou looked at the clock above her stove and replied, "A friend."

Ken allowed himself to breathe. She was going to help him.

She turned slightly from him and spoke into the phone. "I'm glad you're home, can you come right away? No, I'm fine, but I need you here as soon as possible." Before she hung up, she added, "Thanks, Steve."

Ken bolted upright at the name and was rewarded with another stab in his ribs. "You called *Steve?*"

"He can help us."

But he won't, Ken thought. He leaned back in the chair and closed his eyes. He had failed. Nothing would change. Millions would die. Eighty-seven years into the future, New America will resist the tide of Communism and millions more will meet the same fate. Only this time, it will be the democratic continent that would be reduced to uninhabitable rubble.

Lou surprised him by giving him a gentle hug from behind.

Her hair smelled of lilacs. He turned and looked up at her. It was the first time since he had met her that he was not afraid to say what was on his mind. "We have approximately three hours before we become ash. Let's go hide somewhere and make love."

Shock froze her features. Then a grin erupted between flushed cheeks. "As good as that sounds, shouldn't we wait until after Steve drives you to Volk Field?"

He blinked. "You expect Steve to drive me? There's no way he'll believe me."

"No, of course not." She smiled. "But he'll believe me." She casually walked over to the sink and filled the coffeepot. "I'll make him some coffee. I suggest you have some too. We all should have something hot in our bellies before we make that trip."

He almost blurted out that, if by some miracle Steve did agree to take him, she certainly wouldn't be going along but he decided to postpone that argument. "No coffee for me, thanks."

The clock read ten-thirty. Steve would arrive within minutes. But precious time would be eaten up attempting to convince the bull-headed sheriff to drive to Volk Field, if such a feat were even possible.

"How about a soda?" Lou asked.

He nodded absently.

Before she handed it to him, she paused and said, "I phoned the Coca-Cola Company."

He frowned at her.

"Remember when I first saw you, you were looking at the pop machine and said, 'What, no diet'?" Well, I phoned the company and asked if they made a soda that could be used by people on diets. He said they were currently working on a sugar-free soda and expected it to be released early next year. They're going to call it 'Tab' or something like that."

Tab? He had never heard of it. "So?"

"So why were you looking for something that is not available for another year? How could you know every word of a song that had just been released? And how do you know what will happen if you don't stop those planes?"

He looked up at her. "If somehow we manage to stop those planes, I will tell you everything."

Outside, tires slid in the slush.

Steve had arrived.

* * *

Steve's tires pushed slush into piles when he braked. He bounded up the steps and went into the house without knocking. Instinctively, he went to the kitchen.

He halted in the doorway. Wiseass sat at the table.

"Shit!" Steve spit out the expletive.

Ken nodded. "Good to see you too, Sheriff."

"Want some coffee?" Lou looked worried, confused, and happy all at the same time.

"No. What the hell is going on?"

"We need a lift out to Volk Field." Lou said this in the same tone with which she would ask for a lift to the store. She handed Steve a steaming mug and motioned for him to sit.

He didn't, though he did accept the coffee. He placed it on the table in front of him. "Why the hell would you want to go to Volk Field? Have you looked outside?"

"Sit down and Ken will tell you. Come on, Steve. This is important."

He reluctantly pulled off his sheepskin coat and sat down. "Okay, out with it."

He listened. When Ken finished, Steve let a laugh escape. "This is a joke, right?" He looked at Lou. The worry etched on her face sobered him up. He looked back at Ken. "How the hell do you know what's going to happen?"

Ken hesitated, swallowed, then said, "I'm a little psychic."

Steve jerked upright in his chair. "You're a little liar! Jesus Christ, don't you know better than to lie to an officer of the law?"

"I believe him," Lou said. She stood behind Ken, her left hand on his shoulder. The ease at which she did this confirmed Steve's worst fears about their relationship.

Steve squashed that worry and concentrated on their request. He spat out another laugh. "Tell me, Wiseass, why wouldn't Duluth detect the mistake when the alarms go off and call Volk Field?"

Ken didn't flinch. "It's possible they will. But there is no control tower at Volk Field and they will not be able to stop the planes in time."

Steve admitted inwardly that Ken appeared to believe he told the truth. But the story was too preposterous. He countered, "You're crazy."

Ken continued to meet his gaze. "I'm trying to prevent a nuclear war."

"Why don't you just call Duluth or Volk Field and tell them this?"

"They won't believe me. If they did they might try the alarms and the same chain of events could occur, only earlier. Remember, there is no control tower."

Steve rubbed his head. He was tired and so was his brain. He looked at Lou.

"What harm would it do to drive out there and talk to the person in charge?" she asked.

"I have an idea." Steve laced his tone with sarcasm. "Why don't I just phone the commanding officer at Volk Field? Surely they'll listen to the County Sheriff. That way we won't have to haul our asses out into that Canadian weather." He blew out air in an attempt to curb his temper and then strode to the phone.

He halted when he saw the gun. He picked it up.

"What's this?" he asked as he automatically checked it. When he saw it was loaded, he glared at Ken.

"It's a gun." Ken spoke slowly.

"Wiseass! Where the hell did you get it and why the hell is it here?"

Lou stepped into the line of fire. "Mrs. Lacey gave it to him in case he was attacked again."

"Oh, how nice of her." Steve leaned around Lou so he could continue to glare at Ken. "And just who the hell attacked you?"

Lou took another step sideways and blocked Steve's view. "He wants to keep Ken from stopping the planes."

"Jesus, Lou, will you let Wiseass talk?"

Ken stood up and locked eyes with Steve. "I think he's a communist who wants a nuclear war to take place. America suffered a lot of destruction from the conflict."

"*Suffered?* Past tense? You're slipping, Wiseass. Weren't you speaking about the future?"

"I was. I'm not the English teacher here."

Although he knew he could not win a battle of wits with this fellow, Steve continued, "So how does this commie know you're trying to stop the planes? Is he some kind of psychic, too?"

Ken shrugged. "I don't know. They have their ways, I guess."

Steve sighed, then turned, and picked up the phone. He recognized the voice on the line. "Joyce, this is Sheriff Jensen. I need the line. And I'd better not hear anyone listening in, you hear me?" He shook his head in frustration and dialed zero. "Damn party lines!"

"Hello, Bessie? I need to be connected to Volk Airfield. Okay, I'll hold, but try to speed it up, will ya?" He turned to scowl at his audience for lack of something else to do. Bessie finally came back on the line.

"I'm sorry, Sheriff, but I'm having a dickens of a time getting connected out there. I'll try the main switchboard in Madison."

Steve turned his back and blew out more air. Finally Bessie came back on the line.

"I can connect you to the command center in Duluth, will that do?"

"Yeah, that'll do."

After a serious of clicks a young woman's voice came on the line. "Duluth Section Direction Center, how may I direct your call?"

"I want to speak to the officer in charge." Steve turned to smirk at Ken. This would all be straightened out in a minute and then he could go back home and cuddle up with his warm wife.

A deep voice with a no non-sense tone came on the line. "Major Fulker."

Fulker? Steve grinned when he thought about the version of the name the major's inferiors probably used. He forced himself to assume an equally serious tone. "Yes, this is Sheriff Jensen down in Juneau County. I —" Here Steve faltered. How could he explain without sounding like a nut? The newspapers would have a field day with this one and the next election was only ten months away. He swallowed the lump of doubt in his throat. "I have been informed by someone that there may be a problem with your alarm systems."

"I'm sorry, where did you say you were calling from?"

"Mauston. I'm phoning about Volk Field, actually. I've been told that—"

"That we have a problem with our alarms?"

Steve was all too familiar with this type of know-it-all officer. "Yes. But—"

Again the major cut him off. "What kind of problem?"

"Well, with your alarm down here at Volk Field."

"Who told you that?"

"One of the citizens here. A Ken O'Neil." There, Wiseass would look like the nut, not him. Steve would only appear to be a concerned civilian.

"And what exactly did he tell you?"

Steve gritted his teeth at the condescending tone. "He says the alarm at Volk field is wired wrong and the planes could take off by mistake."

"Listen, Sheriff Jenkens, we operate by SIOPs and although I will get the alarms checked, I do not appreciate you letting some fruitcake civilian take up our precious time when the nation is at DEFCON 2. I think you'd better investigate the background of this O'Neil person."

The line went dead before Steve could tell the fellow it was Jensen, not Jenkens. He slammed the phone down and braced himself for the 'I told you so' looks on Lou's and Ken's faces. But when he turned around, they only looked worried.

He shrugged. "He said he'd check into it."

Lou squeezed Steve's arm. "Why don't we drive out to Volk Field and just chat with them until after midnight? What harm could it do?"

He sighed. "Okay, Wiseass, tell me this. Why didn't you just drive yourself out there? Why bother Lou? Or me for that matter?"

"I don't know how to drive."

Steve almost choked on a laugh. What kind of pansy ass was this fellow?

Ken stepped up to him. "It's eleven o'clock. If you're going to drive me, we have to leave now."

Steve stared at him and Ken returned the look, steadily and convincingly. Damn him.

Steve tucked Mrs. Lacey's gun into his belt. "Okay. I'm going to keep this, though. I wouldn't want you shooting one of us by mistake."

Lou grabbed a toque and scarf in addition to her heavy wool coat.

"You're staying here, Lou," Ken said.

"For once I agree," Steve said. "It could get dangerous with two crazies in the same place."

Lou said nothing, but went out and got into the front seat of the squad car.

Steve walked out and stopped her from closing the car door. "C'mon, Lou. Get your ass back in the house."

"No way. You two need a babysitter *and* a translator. Hurry now, we have to get going."

Steve shrugged and shut the door.

Ken looked at him in disbelief. "You're not letting her come?"

"I've learned it's easier not to argue with her." Steve opened the back door. "You get to ride in the back, Wiseass. Hurry up. According to you, you're running out of time."

Though his dark eyes flashed with anger, Ken climbed awkwardly into the back.

Steve revved the engine, turned on the lights and the siren, and pulled out from the curb. When they reached the highway, visibility dropped to zero. He was forced to slow the car to a crawl.

Nobody said anything. Which was unusual for Lou. And absolutely unheard of for Wiseass.

It was all so unreal.

Like a dream.

Or a nightmare.

TWENTY-FIVE

Ken stared out the window. The distance passed much too slowly and the time too quickly. He knew Steve, hunched as he was over the steering wheel, drove as fast as he dared. Large white flakes attacked the headlights and reduced visibility to a few feet. Whenever the back tires spun in the slush, Steve would let up on the gas pedal until he gained control.

Lou turned around and looked at Ken through the grill. Even in the dark interior he could see the questions in her eyes.

The click of Steve's signal light startled him.

"Are we at the turnoff?" Ken asked. He frowned at his watch. Illuminated dials had not been invented yet.

"No, I'm stopping for doughnuts," Steve growled sarcastically. "This one will take us to the road to the airfield."

Ten minutes later, Steve turned onto a dark and narrow road. An easy road along which to plan an ambush.

Ken leaned ahead. "I don't think we should advertise our location to the communist."

But before Ken finished speaking, Steve had killed the police lights. "I need the headlights, unless your psychic powers can steer this car in the dark."

"Who's the wiseass now?" Lou asked, her attempt at humor overridden by the anxiety in her voice.

Steve remained gnarly. "If you two would keep quiet, it'd be easier for me to concentrate on driving."

Ken put his face near the grill and squinted through the windshield. As no metal was allowed within the time chamber, the enemy agent should be unarmed and most likely would not think he would need a weapon to dispose of Ken. Hopefully the man hadn't considered the possibility that his adversary would bring armed reinforcements.

Ken's face planted into the grid as Steve brought the car to an abrupt halt and snapped off the engine and the lights.

Ken's heart thudded. "What?" He could see nothing ahead.

"Shh!"

They listened.

Nothing.

"I thought I saw something," Steve whispered. "Light reflecting off metal." He opened his door. "We've got twenty minutes. I'm going to scout ahead." He pulled up the bottom of his coat and unsnapped his holster.

"Wait," Ken hissed. "Let me go with you."

"Stay here. Both of you." Steve disappeared into the night.

Panic burned in Ken's gut. He managed to keep his voice low. "Lou, let me out."

"Ken, Steve knows what he's doing. We're probably safer here."

"Lou, that man is a Chinese agent from the year 2049. I don't think Steve has met many people like that."

Lou stared at him a moment, then got out and opened the back door. The snow had stopped and the white blanket provided a bit of reflective light from the few stars beginning to appear overhead.

"Stay here," Ken ordered.

"Like hell," she whispered back.

They didn't have time to argue. Two dark forms approached. As they neared, they acquired human shapes. Steve held his hands up in front of him and walked ahead of a man who pointed a rifle at Steve's back.

It was the Chinese agent.

* * *

The moment Ko saw O'Neil, he rapped the sheriff on the head with the butt end of the rifle and pushed him to the side. He then raised the rifle to his shoulder, and took aim.

O'Neil pushed the woman with him to the side and turned to face him. Ko squeezed the trigger. O'Neil flew backwards and landed in the snow. The woman screamed, then crawled over to O'Neil.

"Noooooo," she moaned.

Ko could see the growing stain in the snow beneath O'Neil, but he stepped closer. He had to make sure. "Move aside."

The woman looked up at him and surprised him with a glare and a defiant "No."

Ko shrugged. "I will make sure you don't suffer." He raised the rifle but before he could pull the trigger, he heard a faint sound behind him. He swung about. The sheriff was on his knees, and had pulled out something from his waistband.

Two barks rang out, one slightly ahead of the other. Time slowed.

Heat thrust into Ko's chest. He could feel the cold snow pressing into him but he did not remember falling.

He tried to take in air, but his lungs only rattled. He wanted to sit up, to make sure O'Neil had died, that both Shimira's and China's future would remain unchanged. But his body no longer followed commands.

Darkness encroached his world until one final image remained: Shimira, her eyes saying goodbye, just before the elevator's doors closed.

* * *

Through her tears, Lou watched Steve stagger toward the dark pile that had once been a man. "Damn, he does look like a bit like a commie. Well, now he's a dead commie."

"Steve . . ." Lou managed to force the name past her tear-choked throat.

Steve lumbered over and knelt beside her. He placed three fingers to Ken's neck, then shook his head.

Lou felt all her strength pour into the snow along with Ken's blood.

"Wait," Steve said, "he has a pulse. It's pretty weak though. We'd better get him to the hospital. Help me get him into the back."

Ken was a dead weight. Just as they got him onto the seat a wail tore through the trees and gained in strength. Through the trees ahead, lights winked on.

Ken's eyes flew open. Blood frothed from his mouth and shone darkly against his pale face. He grabbed Steve's collar. "You've got to . . . you've got to stop . . ." His voice trailed off.

"We've got to get you to the hospital," Steve argued.

Ken tightened his grip and pulled Steve's face close to his. "No. . . the planes . . ." His eyes glazed over and he slumped onto the seat.

Steve looked at Lou, undecided. Then he brightened. "Look, there's a truck a few yards off. Must have been how the commie got here. I can take it to Volk Field and you can drive Ken to the hospital."

"I . . ." Lou started to say she couldn't, but this was the only way to save Ken and possibly still prevent the horror he had predicted. She went around and climbed behind the wheel. "What if . . .?"

Steve cut her off. "I'll beep the horn twice when I'm on the way. If I can't get it started . . ." He waved off the end of his sentence and moved forward like a linebacker with a clear line to the opposing quarterback.

By the time she started the car and turned it around, she heard two beeps much too friendly for the circumstances. Steve would stop the planes. She had to get Ken to the hospital.

She revved the engine, spun for a minute and nearly panicked. Then the tires took hold and the car lurched forward. She dared not glance into the back seat where Ken lay ever so still.

* * *

The old truck was George Miller's. Had that commie killed George? Steve shoved that thought aside and focused on the road ahead.

The old truck managed the snow-slicked road easier than his squad car had. Within a minute he was at the gate. No guard was on duty. There didn't appear to be any phones or buttons to push. He blared his horn but it was not audible above the chorus of fighter engines revving up.

"Damn it!" Steve hesitated only a moment before he allowed his temper to propel him into action. "Wiseass had better be right," he muttered as he gunned the engine and rammed the gate.

Off to his left huddled a row of buildings. To his right he saw a multitude of single lights, some of which had already begun to move. He pulled onto the tarmac and nearly ran over a man in uniform.

He braked and the man climbed in.

Before Steve could say anything, the soldier blurted out, "We have to stop those planes! Go!"

Steve floored the gas pedal. The first of the taxiing planes picked up speed and several others in tandem matched it.

"Flash your lights!" the uniform hollered. He rolled down the window and leaned so far out Steve wouldn't have been surprised to see him disappear in a flash of well-polished leather. The uniform waved his cap and yelled.

Steve pushed on the horn and flashed the lights.

Then he did something he hadn't done in a long time. He prayed.

TWENTY-SIX

When Lou reached the highway, she 'used all the goods,' as Steve would say: siren, four-way flashers, and even the rotating red and white lights. The black asphalt was lined with slush. Dirty spray hit the windshield. Just like the night of her accident.

"Lisa?" The barely audible whisper from the back jolted her. Ken was talking to his wife. His dead wife.

"No!" Lou screamed. "You stay with me Ken. Do you hear me? Don't you die on me!"

The few cars on the streets pulled over and she did not stop for lights or signs. She almost missed the turn to the hospital. She didn't realize how fast she was going until she had to fight to bring the car to a halt in front of the emergency doors. Figures in white rushed out.

By the time she climbed out, they were already pulling Ken from the back seat.

"Louise!" She snapped her head around to a familiar voice. Dr. Williams, her family physician.

"Where's the sheriff?"

"Steve's fine. Ken's been shot!"

She could only watch as they put Ken onto a stretcher and wheeled him inside. She tried to follow but Dr. Williams pulled her to a stop.

He leaned so close his large nose was nearly touching hers. "Lou, Ken is being taken care of. Where is Steve? Does he need an ambulance?"

"Steve's fine," she repeated. "He's at Volk Airfield."

"Volk Airfield?"

Lou nodded and pulled against his hand.

Dr. Williams said, "Okay, I'll go check on Ken." He led her to a chair in the waiting room. "You wait here." It was not a request.

The few minutes the doctor was gone passed like hours. Lou stood up quickly when he returned. She did not like what she read on his face.

"Ken has been taken to the operating room." An awful pause. "We're doing everything we can."

A weakness washed through her and she felt nauseated.

"Sit back down before you pass out," Dr. Williams ordered.

She collapsed into the chair. "Will Ken . . . ?" She couldn't finish the sentence.

Dr. Williams shook his head. "We won't know for some time yet. Dr. Foster will talk to you the moment Ken's out of surgery." He paused. "Lou, is there anyone we should be contacting?"

Lou thought a moment. "Maybe Mrs. Lacey . . ."

"Perhaps we'll call her when we know more."

Lou nodded.

"Can you tell me again where Steve is?"

Lou had no energy to even begin to gather thoughts. "Steve will be here soon. He'll tell you."

Dr. Williams frowned. "Okay. We'll come and get you when we know something."

"Please."

The noise of chatter, ringing telephones, and the quick footfalls of a nurse's orthopedic shoes on linoleum meshed into a distant blur.

Midst all the activity, she felt so terribly alone.

* * *

Masked people in gowns huddle around the stretcher. One man in particular works feverishly while the person next to him sticks a plastic tube into the patient's chest.

"More suction!" the active man hollers, though the others are so close he doesn't really need to raise his voice.

The face of the person on the stretcher is partially hidden by the oxygen mask. Ken knows he is the person on the stretcher. Or he was the person on the stretcher.

He senses someone beside him. A hand reaches for him, the palm turned up just like the hand he had seen in the river. He now recognizes that hand: it's gentle swells and curves, the small scar in the center of the palm from when she'd fallen off a bicycle as a child. Even before he fully turns, he knows it is Lisa. Her smile washes warmth through him.

"Hey, Lise." Ken reaches to embrace her but she has no form. He cannot see his arms, either, and he wonders about this.

"It's time for me to go, Ken," she says, though her lips do not move.

"I'm coming too."

She shakes her head and blows him a kiss. Then, like a mist before a breeze, she disappears.

"Wait, I want to go with you."

But he doesn't go anywhere and is left alone to watch what is happening below.

* * *

Lou sat alone in the windowless room with half a dozen padded chairs and a night table stacked with magazines. A black and white "No Smoking" sign stared down at her.

Too bad. For the first time in many years she craved a cigarette.

She had phoned Matt, more to hear his voice and tell him she loved him than to relay the events of the evening. In the end, all she could tell him was that Ken had been shot.

Matt had wanted to come home right away. But she told him there were no buses running that time of night, and there was nothing he could do anyway. She promised she was all right and that she'd call him in the morning.

But she was far from all right. On so many levels. She'd heard nothing that indicated a nuclear war was imminent, no warning for them run to bunkers and cellars. No sirens or explosions. Wouldn't something be happening by now if the planes had taken off?

It had been half an hour since they had brought Ken from the operating room to the intensive care unit. But no one had come to her. Surely they hadn't forgotten she was waiting for news. Then again, no news was better than bad news, she decided.

On both fronts.

She started as the door opened. It was Steve. She instinctively went to him and hugged him.

She leaned back. "You stopped the planes?"

He nodded and she leaned in for another hug. He felt so solid. She wished she could transfer some of his strength to Ken.

Steve let go and looked down at her. "Are you okay?"

She nodded.

"How's Wiseass?"

She shrugged her shoulders and tried not to cry. "No word yet. So . . . no nuclear war?"

Steve grunted. "This has got to be the strangest goddamn night of my life. And after Korea, I never thought that'd be possible. I go out onto the runway and nearly run down the guard. He had gotten a call from Duluth saying the intruder that had set off the alarms had turned out to be a bear. Ken was right, the wiring was wrong at Volk Field and the planes were taking off thinking they were at war.

"When the guard hopped into his jeep to stop the planes, the starter went. He was running on foot toward the runway when I got there. The bombers were taxiing already but we did manage to stop them." Steve's bright eyes reflected the adrenaline still juicing his blood. "It took a while to explain why I was there in the first place."

"What did you tell them?"

He shrugged. "Just what I know, which is not much. I told them Ken had a hunch something was wrong with the alarm. I said the Chinese agent ambushed us and shot Ken. Then I managed to shoot the commie. Then I went to try to stop the planes from taking off. Once the military saw the commie's body, they kinda accepted my story. They gave stern instructions for the three of us not to leave Mauston, especially Ken, and for us not to talk to anyone before they get a chance to debrief us in detail. Good thing I'm the County Sheriff or I don't think they would have let me leave the base."

"Well, I don't think Ken's going anywhere fast." Not physically. And hopefully not spiritually. She lowered her weary body into a chair.

"Have you talked to Matt?" Steve asked.

She nodded. "Only about Ken getting shot. I promised to call him in the morning though heaven knows what I'm going to tell him."

"Tell him the truth." Steve patted her shoulder. "Why don't you go home and get some rest?"

She shook her head. "I can't leave Ken."

Steve sat down opposite her. His broad features sagged as the excitement faded and fatigue seeped in.

"You go home, Steve. I'm fine. I'll call if I need you. Susan will be worried."

"Nah. I already called her. I've sent a couple of guys out to George Miller's farm. That Chinese guy stole George's truck. I hope George is okay."

Dr. Williams opened the door. The long evening was beginning to show on him as well. "Ken is in critical condition and we expect he will remain so for the next while. He's still unconscious. You can see him for a minute." He looked at Steve. "Sorry Sheriff, but I don't think you're the one he'd like to wake up to."

Steve put a hand to his chest as if his heart was broken. Then he winked at Lou. "I'll be at home. Call me."

Lou nodded and focused on the words, 'when he wakes up.'

But when she saw Ken she doubted he ever would. He looked so pale. His right arm was wrapped in tensors and resting on a pillow. A tube went into his mouth and when the machine beside him whirred his chest rose and fell. Another tube poked from under the blankets on the left side of the bed and dripped watery blood into a glass jar set on the floor.

He looked so peaceful.

So not there.

TWENTY-SEVEN

October 27, 1962

Lou couldn't remember when she had felt this tired. Her eyes grew heavy and she slumped down into the chair so her head could rest against the back. Before she allowed her eyes to shut she glanced over at Ken.

His chest rose and fell without the aid of a machine. Last night he had awakened thrashing and in a panic. He only calmed down when she managed to convince him that the planes had been stopped. Later they took him off the respirator and moved him to this private room on the surgical floor.

Since then he had slept most of the time, and only aroused for brief periods long enough to smile, squeeze her hand, or say, "Hey, Lou," before he fell back to sleep.

That morning she had endured a lengthy interrogation at Volk Field. They had tried to haul her away from Ken's side the day before, but she had been adamant about not leaving until Ken's status had been upgraded from critical. If not for Steve's intervention, the men in uniform would have probably taken her by force.

Steve had pulled in every influential friend he could to keep the military bullies at bay. A fishing buddy who happened to be a county judge. The state senator whom he knew from West Point. The Mayor of Mauston.

Someone must have successfully waded through the bureaucracy because when they approached her this morning the demeanor had changed from demanding to downright polite. Without using the word 'psychic', she had told them that Ken had been worried the alarm would go off by mistake and they had asked Steve to drive them to Volk Field. After two hours, the four interrogators appeared satisfied with her lack of knowledge although Steve did warn her she was liable to be tailed until things settled down with the Soviets. And who knew when and if that would ever happen?

She startled when the door opened. Two men in dark suits entered. The small hairs on her neck bristled. "Who are you?"

They did not acknowledge her presence, let alone her question. One parked beside the door. The other methodically went around the room as if looking for something. He lifted the sheets off Ken.

"Hey!" Lou barked.

The man dropped the sheets and checked under the bed. The curtains were lifted and tugged. Through the window he looked up, down, left, and right.

"Who the hell are you?" she yelled.

Lou might as well have been a ghost they couldn't see or hear. The man continued to scan the room. He spent a good two minutes in the bathroom.

When he came out, Lou asked sarcastically, "Did you wash your hands?"

He only nodded at his partner and the two left without speaking.

Lou was about to chase after them when the door opened and in walked President John F. Kennedy.

I'm dreaming, thought Lou. That's it. I'm dreaming.

He smiled at her. "You'd be Mrs. Louise Jensen." His charm enveloped her from across the room.

Her voice did not accompany her into this dream. She could only nod.

The president pointed to the bed. "He's still sleeping?"

Me too, she thought. Again she could only nod.

He smiled again. "Would you mind waking him? I don't have much time."

She forced her wooden legs to carry her to the bed. Without taking her eyes off President Kennedy she reached out and gently jiggled Ken's leg.

Ken's eyes fluttered open. He muttered, "Hey Lou," then shut them again.

She reached toward Ken again but the president held up his hand.

"No. Leave him. He should rest." President Kennedy held her gaze a moment, then his eyes wandered over her. An assessment.

Lou felt a blush warm her cheeks.

"Back off, Jack, she's taken."

Lou jumped back at Ken's words. But by the time she looked down at him his eyes were closed once more.

One of the suits stuck his head in the doorway. "Mr. President?"

"Yes?"

"Three minutes, sir."

President Kennedy nodded and waved him out.

By now Ken's eyes were wide open. "Jesus Christ! John F. Kennedy?"

President Kennedy's dimples deepened as his grin widened. "You were right the second time."

Ken struggled to sit up, coughed, then collapsed back on the bed.

"Easy," said Lou. Her concern for Ken helped normalize the situation.

"Mr. President," Ken managed to spit out. "I-I thought I was dreaming."

"You weren't alone," Lou said.

"Uh – did I say anything inappropriate?" Ken glanced at Lou, his forehead wrinkled with worry.

President Kennedy laughed softly. "Not at all. I don't have much time Mr. O'Neil. I just wanted to thank the man who helped prevent a nuclear accident. We live in perilous times and there's always the chance some son of a –," he glanced at Lou, "gun doesn't get the word." He paused briefly. "They say you claim to have known what was going to happen, that you're psychic."

Ken tried to shrug, then winced in pain.

"Perhaps you could provide some insight as to how this confrontation with the Soviets might turn out."

Ken blinked at him. "No one wins in nuclear war."

President Kennedy nodded. "I agree. I met with the Executive Committee this morning and I have responded to a Soviet proposal that could result in a peaceful resolution."

Ken said nothing, but reached for Lou's hand and gave it a tight squeeze.

"We must get beyond this crisis intact." He looked between Lou and Ken. "Did you know that when written in Chinese, the word 'crisis' is composed of two characters? One represents danger and the other represents opportunity."

"Then this could be an opportunity for world peace." Ken's voice sounded weak.

The president patted Ken's leg and moved to the door. "I have to get going." He swung back and grinned at Ken. "Any last predictions before I leave?"

Lou could not tell if the president asked this in jest or absolute seriousness.

Ken nodded. "History will remember you as one of America's greatest presidents."

Kennedy's grin broadened and his eyes brightened with pleasure. Then without another word, he left the room.

"Now that was a weird dream." Ken's voice was nearly a whisper. He blinked several times. "It wasn't a dream, was it?"

"No. But before you drop off to sleep I need a promise."

He smiled weakly at her. "Yes, I'll marry you."

Blood returned to her cheeks. "That's not what I meant, though I will remind you later you said that. Promise me you'll tell me everything when you're stronger. Everything. Promise?"

He looked at her. "You might not want to marry me if I do."

"I won't marry you *unless* you do."

He squeezed her hand then closed his eyes.

Lou sat back down in the chair. Before she fell asleep, two quietly spoken words came from the bed.

"I promise."

EPILOGUE

November 22, 1963

Ken washed his face for the third time. He looked in the mirror. The repeated dousing of cool water failed to wash away the sorrow. He sighed heavily. At the moment he felt like he had in 2049. Near despair.

He had taken Anna out in her stroller to enjoy the crisp autumn air. When they reached Elm Street a kid selling papers had screamed the news of Kennedy's assassination. Ken rushed home, first insisting he had heard wrong, then praying he had.

The radio informed him the assassin was in custody. By the time he undressed Anna and laid her into her crib, his tears were flowing steadily and dripped off the end of his nose. Anna must have mistaken his wrinkled visage for a smile, because she responded with a wide toothless grin.

She continued to coo while he washed his face once more. He went to her. She smiled when she caught his eye. He picked her up and hugged her close.

The front door opened and Lou entered, her arms laden with groceries. He could tell by her face that she had heard. She set the bags down and came to him. Silently, without a word, they held each other and their child.

Over the next two weeks Ken's grief grew into an anxiety that would stay with him forever. The government selected a commission to investigate the assassination of John F. Kennedy and the subsequent murder of his assassin.

President Kennedy had successfully resolved the Cuban Crisis. He had steered the aggressiveness of the Soviets from an arms race into a space race. He had wanted to remove troops from Vietnam. But immediately after his assassination, his successor reversed this pathway to peace.

Was it possible that the additional shooter that was rumored to be behind the fence along the grassy knoll had been another agent from the future?

This, Ken would never know. What he did know was that the world would continue on its precarious journey through its nuclear minefield of mutually assured destruction. He resolved to continue to speak out against the use of nuclear arms and against American involvement in Vietnam.

He could do little else.

Because he was no longer a player in the telling of time.

AFTERWORD

This novel was inspired by an actual event. The following is a direct quote obtained from Wikipedia concerning Volk Field.

"During the Cuban missile crisis a majority of B-47 bombers with capability to drop nuclear payloads were "dispersed" to Volk, among other bases, to make it harder for the Soviets to threaten USAF assets.[4]

At around midnight on 25 October 1962, a guard at the Duluth Sector Direction Center saw a figure climbing the security fence. He shot at it, and activated the "sabotage alarm." This automatically set off sabotage alarms at all bases in the area. At Volk Field, Wisconsin, the alarm was incorrectly wired, and the Klaxon sounded which ordered nuclear armed F-106A interceptors to take off. The interceptor crews had not been notified that the Strategic Air Command had increased its patrols of nuclear-armed bombers, some of which were airborne near Volk, threatening the possibility of nuclear friendly fire.

Immediate communication with Duluth showed there was an error. By this time aircraft were starting down the runway and Volk was too small for a control tower (its aircraft were dispatched from Duluth 300 miles (480 km) away). A truck raced from the command center and successfully signaled the aircraft to stop.

The intruder was later identified as a black bear, not the Soviet saboteurs in advance of a nuclear attack the sentry was expecting."[5]

(http://en.m.wikipedia.org/wiki/Volk_Field_Air_National_Guard_Base)

ACKNOWLEDGEMENTS

I would like to thank Pat Thomas for encouraging me to revise this novel and publish it. Her suggestions, along with those of my fellow writers in Houston and here in Halifax have been very valuable. Special thanks to my son Dave and my friend Jackson Mitchell for their input.